FOOL'S GOLD

Bill Tucker has spent most of his life being pushed around. When he moves out to Wyoming and buys his own patch of ground, he is determined not to be seen as a small man anymore. But when he discovers gold on his new acres, he draws the attention of Septimus Arkwright, a local cattle company owner. For, blaming the Homestead Act for bringing Tucker to these parts, Arkwright considers the land — and the gold — to be rightfully his . . .

Books by Brent Larssen
in the Linford Western Library:

DEATH AT THE YELLOW ROSE

BRENT LARSSEN

FOOL'S GOLD

Complete and Unabridged

LINFORD
Leicester

First published in Great Britain in 2014 by
Robert Hale Limited
London

First Linford Edition
published 2017
by arrangement with
Robert Hale
an imprint of
The Crowood Press
Wiltshire

*A catalogue record for this book is available
from the British Library.*

ISBN 978–1–4448–3487–1

Published by
F. A. Thorpe (Publishing)
Anstey, Leicestershire

Set by Words & Graphics Ltd.
Anstey, Leicestershire
Printed and bound in Great Britain by
T. J. International Ltd., Padstow, Cornwall

This book is printed on acid-free paper

Prologue

1833

The rain showed no signs of letting up; if anything, it was getting heavier. And to crown it all, lightning had begun flickering on the horizon. A regular storm was brewing up and heading his way. The solitary traveller plodded along through the downpour on his horse. If he didn't find shelter soon, he thought to himself, he was going to be mighty cold and wet by nightfall.

For the last three months, he had been working his way south along the foothills of the Stony Mountains and had finally struck lucky just four days earlier. It was the richest seam of gold he had ever heard tell of and it was all his. In his pack was a leather bag containing over a pound of little pieces of gold, ranging in size from a melon seed to something as big as a small pea. Having picked up as much as he could, the man had covered up all traces of his prospecting and was now heading down east towards the Great Plains. He had it in mind to use what he had so far collected to finance a proper expedition in the summer. But now, here he was, stuck in the open and probably a good thirty miles from the nearest habitation. He would catch the pneumonia at this rate.

Ahead was a rocky bluff, which towered above the surrounding grassland. With the vague notion of finding a cliff which might provide some protection from the lashing rain, the man urged his horse on into a canter. As he neared the rocky mass, something interesting caught his eye. A stream ran towards the bluff and the man thought that he could see something akin to a little cave, nestling in the bank of the stream. Nearby was a huge, dead tree.

The man reined in and dismounted, taking his pack, with its precious contents with him. He tied the horse to a branch jutting out from the dead tree and then slithered down the mud to the little cave he had spied. To his delight, he found that it was bone dry within and he gratefully crept in, out of the torrential rain.

There was barely room for him to squeeze into the place, which was really little more than a large hole in the earth and rocks which lined the course of the stream. But at least it was dry. He was dying for a smoke, but had run out of tobacco a few days previously. Instead, the man fumbled in his pack and drew out the bag which held the gold he had unearthed. Even in the shadowy confines of the cave, with evening drawing near, the chunks of metal gleamed brightly. He took out a few of the larger lumps and caressed them lovingly. This would change his life forever.

While he gloated over his good fortune, the thunder grew louder and the storm swept on until it was directly overhead. The tall old tree to which he had hitched his horse could not help but act as a positive magnet for the lightning bolts which were licking the plain. The first that the man knew of his danger was a flash of vivid blue light which lit up the interior of the cave. At almost the same moment, there was a horrible splintering noise, followed by a crack of deafening thunder. A sudden panic seized him and the man half rose to his feet before the huge tree came crashing down upon his shelter. The weight of the tree caused the hole in which he was hiding to collapse, burying him under tons of rock and soil. The bag he had been holding flew from his hands and some of the contents scattered in and around the stream.

The man was crushed beneath the combined weight of the tree and all the rock which now pinned him down. Earth filled his mouth and he was too badly injured even to cry out. As he lay helpless, with less than a quarter hour of life remaining to him, the rain washed the pieces of gold down into the mud of the river bank, until they slid into the water and were lost to view.

1

It sometimes seemed to Bill Tucker that he had spent the whole of his forty-two years being pushed around by nigh-on every person he met, and treated constantly like a man of no account. When he had claimed his quarter section under the Homestead Act, one hundred and sixty acres of his very own to farm, Tucker had believed that he would be starting on equal terms with all the other pioneers who were moving to that corner of Wyoming in the spring of 1874. But no, wouldn't you just know it? His land was quite different from that of his fellow homesteaders who had joined the rush. It was almost as though the Lord Himself had looked down upon the Earth and said, 'Hmmm, something's not right here! That Bill Tucker is getting to be a bit above his self, expecting to have the same as other folks got. I'd better remind him that his lot is always to find himself at a disadvantage compared to those around him.'

It was crazy to think so of course, but as soon as he set eyes on the land allotted to him, Bill Tucker knew that he had, yet again, drawn the short straw. By the time that Tucker took up his rights, the more fertile and hospitable parts of the Great Plains had already been settled. So it was that his allocation of land was in a bleak corner of the territory, almost in the foothills of the Rocky Mountains. Even so, he was not alone in moving to that area at just that time and he might reasonably have expected to start on equal terms with everyone else. But whereas every other settler for miles around had a hundred and sixty acres of virgin grassland that could be ploughed up as soon as they pleased, Bill Tucker found when he arrived that he had only half as much arable land as his neighbours. The greater part of eighty acres of the hundred and sixty he had been allocated were taken up not by grass-land, but by a huge, craggy outcrop of bare rock. This bluff was visible for miles around and acted as somewhat of a landmark for those travelling in the area.

'You surely been sold a pup there, boy, and no mistake,' observed the first of his near neighbours to whom he spoke after unhitching his oxen from the wagon and preparing to build his soddie. 'Yes sir, you been well cheated.'

'Well,' said Tucker, 'you might say so. Still and all, you got to play the hand you're dealt and not the one you'd wish for. Most likely, somebody back east has a big map and has just drawn a grid over it and divided it up into sections. Stands to reason, 'less you come out here, you wouldn't o' known of this here pile of rock, plumb bang in the middle of this area. It's the luck o' the draw.'

Tom Logan, the man who had dropped by to commiserate with Tucker over his ill fortune, was impressed and irritated in equal measure with his neighbour's stoical acceptance of a situation which might have driven a lesser man to drinking, cursing and who knew what-all else. Had he been around the following morning when Tucker began ploughing, he might have found the man considerably less philosophical about matters.

The first thing anybody moving to virgin land of that sort did on arriving was to build a place to live. If there were trees nearby, then they might put up some kind of log cabin, the sort of house where Abe Lincoln was raised. Otherwise, they would need to build a soddie. This was a single-story building constructed of turf. The earth in that grassland, which had never been ploughed since the world began, was not crumbly and loose like the soil in a cultivated garden. It was a densely packed mass of roots, which mean that when first ploughed, a long cable was turned over, which could be cut into sections to build walls with. It was a primitive but effective way of throwing up a home in a week or so.

Bill Tucker harnessed his shiny new plough up to the oxen which had pulled his wagon the five hundred miles he had travelled to get to Wyoming. Two minutes after he began to plough, Tucker was compelled to stop, because the blade of the plough had stuck behind a boulder buried a few inches below the surface. It was pretty much the same story, wherever he ploughed. Over the course of the years, the rock of the bluff had been split by lightning and frost, worn away by rain and eroded by windborne dust. Huge chunks of rock had been scattered all over the surrounding area and gradually sunk into the soil. It would be a nightmare, trying to cultivate this land and convert it into arable, crop-producing fields.

However accustomed you might have become over the years to disappointment and the dashing of your hopes, and Bill Tucker was more familiar with such feelings than most, there still comes a time when you feel a mite put out by the way that the world uses you. Tucker unharnessed the plough and turned the oxen loose to graze. Then he walked slowly up to the bluff. His path took him along the stream which ran right up to the rocky face, before vanishing into a sinkhole.

It was a gloomy and overcast morning which made the flash of light from the bed of the stream all the more noticeable. At first, Tucker thought it might have been a fish, but in that case, the glint would surely have been silvery? He had the idea that there had been a yellowish tinge to what he had momentarily glimpsed. It was not until he had gone right up to the edge of the stream that he had been able to see what had caught the light. It looked to him like a little yellow pellet, laying in the mud over which the shallow water flowed. Tucker stepped into the stream, bent down and plucked up the object.

Back on the bank, he examined carefully the piece of metal which he had retrieved. He guessed that it was probably pyrites, what they called 'fool's gold'. It was heavy though, weighing — as far as Tucker could gauge — about as much as a lead bullet of similar size might. He rubbed his jaw thoughtfully.

★ ★ ★

'Where did you say you found this?' asked Mr Halliday. The walk to town had taken Tucker nearly two hours, but it seemed to him that it might be time well spent. Jubilee Falls was not a big place, but there were several stores, including Halliday's General Provisions. Carl Halliday, a genial old fellow, bought and sold all manner of goods. Many of the new settlers didn't have a whole heap of cash money, but most had brought with them various heirlooms and articles which could be disposed of for money: clocks, watches, jewellery, items of furniture, crockery, books and all manner of other goods. Halliday would buy practically anything or, if it was preferred, barter it for goods in his store.

On his way to the land on which he was planning to settle, Bill Tucker had stopped over in Jubilee Falls and visited Halliday's store. He remembered the second-hand jewellery that he had seen there and the memory had put it into his head that Mr Halliday might be able to tell him about the little chunk of metal which he had picked up from the stream. Here was a man who would surely be able to recognize real gold when he saw it.

'I picked it up from the stream which runs through my property,' said Tucker, not seeing any good reason to dissemble. 'Thought you might be able to tell if it's gold or just pyrites. Fool's gold, you know.'

'I know all about fool's gold. There's a lot of it round here and I sometimes get men coming in here, sure they've struck rich, when all along they just hit upon a heap of iron pyrites. You want to know how to tell the difference 'tween the two?' asked Halliday. 'There's no great art to it. Lookee here now.' He took a pair of pliers from beneath the counter and then placed the piece of metal between the jaws and squeezed gently. He showed the result of this action to Tucker; the yellow lump was squashed and distorted. 'Now watch,' said Halliday. He took another little lump of yellow metal from a shelf behind him and repeated the process. This time, it shattered into fragments as soon as he applied pressure.

Bill Tucker scratched his head. 'Does that mean as that's gold, meaning the bit I brought here?'

'Means it ain't pyrites, anyways.'

'Is that what you do to rings and earbobs, when you're trying to see if they are made of gold?'

The old man chuckled. 'Lord, no. T'wouldn't be no manner of use bending and squashing items like that. 'Sides which, other stuff as looks like gold can be soft too.' He reached into a little cabinet behind him and brought out a pocket watch. He handed it to Tucker, saying, 'Here, what do you make to this here?'

Tucker took the watch in his hands and turned it over. It was made of smooth, gleaming yellow metal. He looked up at Halliday and said, 'Is this gold?'

'Not a bit of it,' replied Halliday, a broad smile on his face. He was evidently enjoying his little lecture and since this was stuff that Bill Tucker wanted to know about, he saw no cause to interrupt Halliday. The old boy continued. 'This is made of Pinchbeck metal, which is a mixture of copper and zinc. Looks just like gold, don't it? Some folks, they carry Pinchbeck watches and jewellery when they're travelling by stage. They get held up by road agents, all they lose is cheap imitations, not the real thing. You can bend this stuff with pliers, it won't shatter like pyrites.'

'So how can you tell if something is solid gold?' asked Tucker patiently.

'Look here. I got a little bottle here of stuff they call Aqua Fortis, which is Latin for strong water. You ever hear of it?'

'No, I don't mind that I did.'

'Well, we can test your piece of metal for certain sure using this stuff.' The old man took a piece of black stone from a drawer beneath the counter. 'Now watch. I rub your metal on this and it leaves a little streak of yellow behind. Now it could be Pinchbeck or other stuff. All we know so far is that it's a yellow metal.'

'If you say so,' said Tucker, thinking privately that Carl Halliday must be one of the wordiest men he had ever encountered.

'Now, I pour this Aqua Fortis on the mark on the stone and what do we see?'

'Nothing,' said Tucker. 'It ain't made any difference.'

'Which means that this here is pure gold!' said Halliday triumphantly.

Well, thought Tucker, they'd had to chase round the woodpile for a spell, but they had eventually arrived at their destination.

'How much is this worth?' he asked.

Old man Halliday brought out a little balance that he used when buying jewellery and placed the gold in one pan. After a little tinkering around, he announced, 'This is a shade over half an ounce. Shall we say eight dollars?'

Tucker took the money and went off in something of a daze. Halliday had expressed the desire to be given first option on any other gold that was unearthed on Tucker's land.

* * *

At about the same time that Bill Tucker was leaving Halliday's General Provisions Store, Septimus Arkwright was sitting on the porch of his house, gazing moodily out towards the distant horizon. He had been sitting there, brooding, for almost an hour. There were two problems on his mind; the one a longstanding one and the other a sharp and immediate danger to him.

Ten years earlier, the Arkwright Cattle Company had been the biggest outfit for many miles around. Arkwright's herds had unlimited grassland on which to graze and no shortage of water either. That year, before the outbreak of war in 1862, Arkwright had been a big man, a man of standing, a man that few would wish to cross. Even during the War between the States, he had still done pretty well and his company had secured a number of valuable contracts. It was after 1866 when things began to go wrong. The actual cause of his woes had begun in 1862 with the passing of that damned Homestead Act. Mind, for the next four years, most folk had been too busy prosecuting the war to worry overmuch about moving west and starting farms out in Nebraska and Wyoming, but after the surrender, there had begun a steady trickle of optimistic families to the open lands in the west. By the late 1860s, the trickle had become a torrent and the Arkwright Cattle Company was in deep trouble.

The government in Washington believed that nobody owned the land that they were so free and easy about handing out to anybody who had fought on their side in the war. For men like Arkwright though, it meant the loss of a vital resource; the wide spaces needed to tend for their herds. Every new settler meant one more patch of grassland which was not available for Arkwright's steers to roam. These families, who Septimus Arkwright thought of as 'squatters', were strangling his business with their fences and fields.

In recent weeks, Arkwright had been putting in motion plans to tackle this longstanding grievance. It was apt to be a bloody business, but then so was lancing an abscess. Sometimes, blood needed to be spilled before things could get better.

The immediate concern for Arkwright though was not the squatters who were slowly choking his herds off from the pastures and water that they needed to survive. It was connected to that question, but was a sight more urgent.

As a direct consequence of his difficulties with those settling on his land, or what he at any rate regarded as his land, Arkwright had found that he had a temporary problem with liquidity; which was to say that he couldn't raise the money needed for wages and such like. His solution was to approach a bank, not in Jubilee Falls but further east in South Pass City. He had never had any difficulty with such transactions in the past, but maybe the bank didn't view the Arkwright Cattle Company as the safe and solid concern that it had once been.

They would only advance him the necessary funds in exchange for a mortgage on his ranch. He hadn't been overjoyed about it, but needs must when the Devil drives. This had been nearly a year ago and Arkwright had managed to pay back nearly all the money; all bar three thousand dollars, that is to say. And there was the rub.

There had never been any trouble about holding back on creditors before, but when Arkwright looked at the fine print of the mortgage, he saw that if every cent had not been repaid in full by the due date — that due date being within three weeks of now — the ranch and all its land would become the property of the First National Bank. If he could not come up with that sum in the next twenty-one days and somehow get it to the bank in South Pass City, he would be ruined.

* * *

On the way back to his land, Tucker passed by Tom Logan's spread. Logan hailed him and asked what was what.

'I don't rightly know,' said Tucker. 'You ever hear aught about gold being found hereabouts?'

'I ain't been here above two months, myself,' Logan reminded him, 'but no, nobody said anything like that. Why'd you ask?'

It was on the tip of Bill Tucker's tongue to open up to the other man, but at the last moment, he thought the better of it. Instead, he said, 'I dunno. With the state of that land I got, I wondered if digging for gold wouldn't be a better bet than planting corn.' At which, Tom Logan burst out laughing. You had to admire a man like that, he thought, who met his reverses so cheerfully and without complaint. Even so, Logan felt obscurely cheated by the exchange. It is galling when you have geared yourself up to sympathize with a man and maybe patronize him a little too, to find that he is coping just fine with his misfortune.

It was needless for Bill Tucker to have been so coy about the details of his discovery, because Carl Halliday had no such inhibitions. In the Star of the West saloon that very evening, he was giving chapter and verse to anybody who had ears to listen. 'Yes siree,' he said, 'a nugget weighing at just over half an ounce. Said he picked it right out o' that stream as runs through his land, nigh to Indian Bluff.'

'You think there's more?' asked a loafer at the bar.

Halliday enjoyed his reputation locally as a man who knew about most everything. He was surely gaining vicarious pleasure from Tucker's good fortune and felt inclined to talk up that man's likely prospects.

'I should say so,' he said confidently. 'Happens all the time. Why, just look at South Pass City, how that grew up from just such a chance strike. The lay of the land is similar there to what it is here. Yes, I would say that there is more gold to be found there for sure.'

One of those listening to the conversation at the bar that evening happened to be Septimus Arkwright's foreman, Jed Stone. He listened carefully to the whole of what was said and then slipped unnoticed from the barroom. This was something that his boss would want to know about at once. Stone was deep in Arkwright's counsels and he knew that there was an urgent need for money. This might be the very thing. It could also tie in with certain plans that had already been laid, with a view to clearing some of the newcomers from the land which they were on. It was time to halt and then perhaps reverse the flow of immigrants to this corner of the territory.

2

The day after visiting town, Bill Tucker decided that however arduous, he should start work on that soddie of his. He didn't much feel like spending too many more nights sleeping under the wagon. Before he harnessed up the oxen though, he wanted to take another look at that stream.

Like most people who had heard about the gold rushes in places like California, Tucker knew vaguely about 'panning for gold'. What this might in practice entail though, was quite beyond him. They say that doing something is often the best way of learning and so when he went up to the stream, Tucker took with him a chipped china plate, which was the entirety of his crockery. You had to start somehow.

Peering into the water near to where he had picked up the piece of gold the previous day revealed no other obvious signs of gold and so Tucker took off his boots, rolled up his pants and waded into the stream. It was a shallow little waterway; less than two foot deep. He bent down and scooped up some sand and mud on his plate and then let the current sweep most of it away. By turning the plate this way and that, Tucker soon found that he could let the silt be carried away, leaving only stones behind.

At first, nothing at all was left when all the grit and sand had been washed away; just ordinary little pebbles and stones. Tucker thought it worth trying at the exact spot where he had picked up the bit of gold the day before. This spot was easy enough to find, because it was right where an old tree trunk lay at right angles to the stream.

As soon as he began at this new location, his luck changed. When he lifted the cracked old plate from the water, he saw at once that it was not only stones which remained, caught by the lip of the plate. There were also two little yellow lumps; nuggets, he supposed that they were called. They were smaller than the piece he had found yesterday, but all the same, he suspected that they too were solid gold. An hour's panning dredged up three more little bits, one of which was almost as big as the nugget for which Halliday had given him eight dollars.

It has to be said that Bill Tucker was not a deep thinker and nor was he a quick one. Figuring things out generally took him a mite longer than it did most folks and then like as not he would get the answer wrong anyway. But this time, he was determined to reason out the case to himself and see how things stood. Nearby was the decayed trunk of a mighty tree, which must have been laying here for many years, judging by the lichen and moss which covered it. Part of this overhung the bank of the stream. Tucker clambered out of the water and sat astride the old tree trunk to work out how matters stood.

There was no doubt at all that this land was his and that any minerals found on it belonged exclusively to him. That was the first point. Nobody could come along here and try and stake a claim to this stream and its contents. That was a comforting thought. Next off was where he had the leisure to work at this as though that was his livelihood. Yesterday, he had received enough to keep him in vittles for a week. Like as not, what he had fished out of the water today would fetch at least the same again. At this rate, he would be able to live on the proceeds of his prospecting.

These pleasant reflections were interrupted by the arrival of two men on horses. By the look of them, they were hard ones and Tucker had the distinct impression that they wanted to speak to him.

★   ★   ★

When he had got back to the Double D after leaving the saloon so precipitately,

Jed Stone had found his boss in a foul mood. He was cursing a couple of cowboys whom he accused of screwing something up. For all that Septimus Arkwright liked to represent himself these days as a sober and respectable, middle-aged businessman he was swearing like a drunken mule skinner. The two boys were too cowed to do anything other than listen meekly to the abuse. When Arkwright caught a sight of Stone, he called him over. 'Well? What's happening in town?'

'Let's walk aways over here, boss.'

When they were out of earshot of the cowboys, Arkwright said again, 'Well?'

Stone told him what he had heard in the Star of the West and Arkwright grew thoughtful. He hooked his thumbs into his belt and beat a nervous tattoo upon the leather with his fingertips. At length, he said, 'What d'you make of it?'

Stone shrugged and said slowly, 'No reason why it shouldn't be a true bill. There's gold hereabouts. Not much, but no reason why there shouldn't be a seam on that patch of land.'

'What's your gut feeling?' asked Arkwright.

'I'd say that that squatter has set his self down on a reef of gold. Can't see any other explanation.'

'Well then,' said Arkwright. 'We'll just have to see if we can prise him off the place. Clock's ticking, Jed. You know as well as I do, that if we don't get that money to the bank on time, we'll all be ruined and you'll be back to being one more lonely saddle-tramp.'

The next morning, Arkwright and Stone decided to be neighbourly and pay Tucker a little visit. They had no aim of causing trouble at that point, rather they wanted to see what sort of man they would have to deal with if he cut up rough and wouldn't see reason.

* * *

Tucker saw coming towards him that morning an older-looking man with a neatly trimmed grey moustache and a fellow of about thirty, who had one of the meanest faces that Bill Tucker had ever set eyes upon. He stood up to greet the strangers, feeling that it would be ill-mannered to remain slouched on an old log if he was meeting for the first time some of those who lived in this area.

'Good morning to you,' said Tucker cheerfully. 'Goin' to be fine day by the look of it.'

'Yes,' said the older of the two riders, 'I believe that you are right about that, Mr . . . ?'

'Tucker,' he said, striding forward to grasp their hands, 'Bill Tucker.'

'Septimus Arkwright,' said the man with the grey moustache, while the younger man just said, 'Stone'.

'We heard that you had some luck,' said Arkwright. 'Found gold here, they say.'

'Lordy,' exclaimed Tucker. 'News surely does travel fast in these parts. It's no more than twenty-four hours since it happened.'

'Well, to tell you the truth, Mr Tucker,' said Arkwright pleasantly, 'I've lived round here for so long that I feel a kind of fatherly interest in goings on.'

This struck Bill Tucker as a rum thing to say; the stranger not looking to him to be more than five or six years older than he was himself. He waited to see what would follow next.

'You been looking for more gold?' asked Arkwright casually, indicating with a nod the plate that he could see on the log. 'Find anything?'

'A few little bits, nothing to speak of.'

'Well, we'll be getting along. Congratulations on your luck, my friend.'

After the two men had gone, Tucker thought over the exchange and could not help thinking that there was something odd about it. Why should two complete strangers ride all the way out here just to congratulate him on his good fortune? Something didn't ring true.

As they rode back to the Double D, Arkwright said to his foreman, 'What d'you think? You reckon there's gold there?'

'What else? If he's finding bits of the stuff every day, there must be a good sized reef in the vicinity.'

'How come nobody else has struck it then?'

'That's no mystery. I seen such things happen up in Montana. You know I did a bit of prospecting myself in my younger days?'

'I don't want to hear your life's history,' said Arkwright irritably. 'All right then, what did you see in Montana?'

'See how that stream of Tucker's rises from one sinkhole and then disappears into another? Same thing can happen with a seam o' gold. It goes along far under the ground and then, for no reason that you can see, pops up to the surface and then dives back underground again. Happen that's what's doin' there with the gold-bearing rock. Means it's limited to that small part of the area.'

'Here's the question, Jed. If a team of men worked flat out for two weeks on that stream and the surrounding land, you think they could find three thousand dollars' worth of gold?'

'Hard to say, boss,' said Stone. 'If there is a reef of gold rises to the surface there, then they surely might. How much would we need?'

Arkwright was silent as he did some simple calculations. Then he said, 'Twenty dollars an ounce, means we'd need a hundred and fifty ounces to make the full three thousand. Reckon it can be done in a couple of weeks?'

'It may be so,' said the other, dubiously.

'It's cutting it awful fine, but we need to push on with that other thing we talked about. I want Tucker off there within a few days. What do you make of him? As a man, I mean.'

Jed Stone's lip curled contemptuously. 'He's a weakling. Kind of fellow used to being picked on. I don't reckon there'll be any problem dealing with him when the time comes.'

After his visitors had left, Bill Tucker set to with the ploughing again. It was backbreaking and dispiriting work, but he succeeded by the end of the day in turning over a few cables of soil. These, he cut into lengths of two feet or so with a wood saw. He marked out the shape of a hut on the ground with some string and then began humping the blocks of turf into position. By the end of that first day, he had raised the walls to chest height. It had been exhausting, but he was hopeful of finishing them the next day, God willing.

★ ★ ★

Speaking generally, the citizens of Jubilee Falls were pretty evenly divided between those who welcomed the homesteaders and looked to them for the future and another party who were happy with the way things were and thought that the cowboys provided enough money for the town to flourish.

This faction was led by the owner of the Star of the West and also the Madame of the cat house.

There was no denying that the boys from the Arkwright Cattle Company spent pretty freely when they were in town and that this money percolated through the economy of Jubilee Falls, contributing to the general prosperity of the place. The disadvantage was that the cowboys were a pretty rough crew and that they were interested principally in getting liquored up and fighting. The town tolerated this because of the money they brought in.

The homesteaders did not have so much ready cash, but what they did have, they spent in town on things such as lamp oil, seeds, zinc pails, brooms and kitchen utensils. They also provided good business for the blacksmith. There was a smith and forge out at the Double D, so the smithy in Jubilee Falls didn't get a whole lot of custom from that direction.

There had for some time been rumours

about impending trouble between the ranch and the settlers, because you didn't have to think too hard about it to see that there really wasn't room for both in the grasslands around Jubilee Falls. Every day, it seemed like new folk were arriving and as the fences went up, the vast herds which had been in the habit of grazing where they wished were restricted to an ever smaller area. Something had to give and soon.

When they got back to the ranch, Arkwright opened up about the way his mind was working. 'It appears to me,' he said, 'that we can, as you might say, kill two birds with one stone here. We want to put the fear of God into those wretches who have taken the land. We want, too, to work that stream and dig up all the gold laying there.'

'Then what?' asked Stone. 'What do you say we should do?'

The answer was straight and to the point. 'We kill that Tucker fellow,' said Septimus Arkwright. 'We kill him, seize his land and it'll both gain us the money we need right now and also act as a warning to those other squatters.'

* * *

Bill Tucker had been shoved round and looked down upon for the whole course of his life. This had even been the case during the four years that he spent in the army during the war. Some men are like that; other folk just read them as being the type who can be bullied and pushed aside. It is almost like they bear on their brows the mark of Cain; something which signals bullies and everybody else that here is a person who may be mistreated with impunity. The funny thing was that when he was in the army, Tucker had a very specialized and responsible job which you might have thought would earn him some little respect. For Bill Tucker had been an expert on the use of guns and explosives. He had an uncanny knack for handling and using both gunpowder and nitroglycerin and his skill in that field had been famous throughout pretty much the entire Union army. It hadn't been enough though, to stop the bullying.

When he had finished for the day and turned loose the oxen, Tucker tried to think about the next step he should take. So far, he had found little bits of gold just laying there. He had no idea how much more there would be like that, but he would start working the stream bed systematically. He knew nothing about geology, but common sense told him that the little nuggets that he was picking up must have broken off some larger mass. It was logical to assume that this big body of ore must be towards the source of the stream and that the pieces he had found had been carried along by the current and deposited where he had found them. If his reasoning was correct, then after he had picked up all the little pieces of gold in the stream, he would have to look for the rock which contained the ore from which those bits had broken off.

This was the sort of work that Bill Tucker enjoyed — a simple, practical task with a solution that lay in the application of physical force and was not subject to the vagaries of human nature. Tucker had always found people hard to figure and was happiest when working with things rather than people. In this case, the job in hand should entail doing just exactly what he knew best, which was blowing things up. Because if there really was a bunch of gold trapped in some rock, the neatest and most economical means of freeing it would surely be by the use of explosives.

* * *

Septimus Arkwright was not a man to hang back once he had decided definitely upon some course of action. He wanted Tucker dead and what's more, for his purposes, the death needed to be very public and unmistakably brutal. Arkwright wanted every single person camped out on those grasslands in their mud huts to know that one of their number had been mercilessly disposed of. He wanted them all to ask themselves: could I be the next victim? Once you are going to act, there's little point in delay.

* * *

Tucker had two other visitors that same day, shortly after he had finished working on his soddie and before the sun had dipped below the horizon; Tom Logan, in the company of a fellow he introduced as Andy Fisher. The two men arrived on foot and at first there seemed no obvious purpose for their dropping by.

Logan said, 'Hey Tucker. This here is Andy Fisher, who lives over the way. He wanted to meet you.'

'Meet me?' asked Tucker in surprise. 'It's nice to see you Mr Fisher, but why did you want particular to see me?'

'Heard you struck gold here. Wanted

to look round and get the measure of things,' said Fisher.

'Begging your pardon,' said Tucker politely, 'but I'm not sure I follow. Why'd you want to look round my land?' He was plain astounded at how fast the news of his find seemed to be spreading.

'We might be able to help,' explained Tom Logan. 'If you got gold here, it won't be an easy task to dig it up. We could form a group and all work together.' He winked at Tucker and said, 'You're a right sly-boots. You never said a word of this when we met yesterday and all along, you're sitting on your own gold mine!'

Even for a man who was used to having others try and ride roughshod over him and take advantage, this barefaced attempt to muscle in on his claim fairly took Bill Tucker's breath away. He did not want to fall out with his neighbours and so said tactfully, 'Well now, that's mighty nice of you both to offer to help, but I reckon I'm able to handle the business without any assistance. But should I run into difficulties, you can be sure I'll call on you two for help.'

'It's no trouble,' said Logan, laughing. 'We want to help.'

'Like I say,' replied Tucker, 'I'll let you boys know if I should find the job beyond me.'

* * *

Up at the Double D, Septimus Arkwright was speaking quietly and confidentially with Stone. 'You think you can take him tonight?'

'Sure. He's soft as shit. I know the type.'

'We got to make it plain that his death was no accident. It's time to start putting the bite on those bastards who are camping out in our back yard. They need to know that it's time for them to pack up and leave.'

'I'll go by at about one tonight,' said Stone. 'He's sleeping under the stars, ain't yet built his hut. Like as not, I'll be able to slit his throat while he's asleep.'

'Don't leave any sort of sign,' said Arkwright. 'Those others will know all right what's behind it, without any clues. 'Specially once we move in and start digging.'

'Think that vigilance committee in town will take it amiss?'

'No, I wouldn't have thought so. It's not like it's something happening in their town. It wouldn't do for there to be too many such deaths, but one murder won't arouse their interest. Just make it neat, Jed. Know what I mean?'

★   ★   ★

So it was that a little after midnight, Jed Stone set out to pay a visit to Bill Tucker. He had undertaken jobs of this kind before for his boss, all done very quietly and without a deal of fuss. Stone knew that if they didn't take some serious action and pretty damned soon, it was quite true what Arkwright had said. He, Jed Stone, would just become another wretched saddle-tramp, drifting from town to town in search of work. He didn't think that he could face that life again; he was getting too old for it. If avoiding such a fate meant killing a man, stealing his gold and then scaring all those squatters off the Double D's land, then so be it.

In the moonlight ahead, he could see Indian Bluff, rearing up above the plain. The land surrounding the bluff was marked out in little fields and lengths of fencing. Another year, two at the most, and it would no longer be possible to graze any cattle at all round here. The Arkwright Cattle Company would be finished. Well, not while he had breath in his body. Stone had been riding high with Arkwright for several years now and he wasn't about to see it all fall apart because a bunch of little men had descended on the district like a plague of locusts. Tonight was when the fight-back began.

3

Bill Tucker couldn't sleep at all. He settled down beneath the wagon and wrapped himself up nice and cozy in a blanket, but sleep just would not come. He tossed and turned for an hour or more before giving it up as a bad job and getting up again.

The moonlight streamed down upon the landscape, it would have been bright enough to read a newspaper by, had he had such an article to hand. Then it struck him. If he wasn't going to sleep, then he might as well use his time profitably. He went over to the wagon and foraged about until he found the storm lantern. The way that Tucker had figured it earlier was that the gold, if there was a mass of it, must be embedded in rocks. Perhaps the next day, he would examine the bluff itself and see if there was any indication in the rocks there of the presence of gold. But the pieces that he had so far dredged from the stream must, he thought, have come from the other end of it. After all, it flowed towards the bluff, not away from it.

The stream ran for only a quarter mile or so on the surface; emerging from one sinkhole and vanishing into another, right against the bluff. The sinkholes were like the entrances to miniature caves, made of limestone. The aperture from which the water issued was set in the hillside and only about four or five feet high, but Tucker thought that it might be possible for him to work his way along it a little and see if there was any sign of gold. He lit the storm lantern and set off towards the stream.

The cave was slightly larger than he had thought. He would be obliged to crouch down in an uncomfortable fashion, but there was no doubt that he would be able to work his way along for a space. There was one thing; this was the sort of job which was as easily undertaken at night as it would be during the day. Tucker took off his boots and waded into the icy water. Then he started making his way into the cave.

At pretty much the exact same moment when Bill Tucker vanished from sight into the sinkhole, Stone came round the bluff on his horse. He dismounted and then led the horse along at a slow walk. He didn't want to make too much noise and disturb his prey. He had always hated a fair fight. When he was a little closer to the half-built soddie, he slipped a thin, razor-sharp knife from a sheath at his belt and peered at the wagon, to see if he could discern a sleeping figure.

The cave opened out a little as Tucker moved along it. He kept examining the ceiling and walls for signs of gold, but there didn't look to be anything of the kind. He was on the point of going back, when he found that he was in a larger chamber. The walls were smooth and worn and the ceiling was three feet or so above his head. Tucker held up the lamp and then gasped in wonder.

Jed Stone was mightily ticked off by the turn of events. He had searched the area thoroughly and there was no doubt at all that the man he was seeking was not to be found. He toyed with the idea of burning his belongings and knocking down the half-built soddie, but couldn't see that that would accomplish his purpose. He hated it when things went wrong. It made him angry and when Stone got angry, it usually meant that somebody was apt to get hurt.

The cave in which Tucker was standing was like something from a fairy story. He couldn't reach as high as the ceiling, not even to brush with his fingertips, but in the light of the lamp, he could see that it was glittering with yellow light. A broad seam of ore swept from one side of the cave roof to the other and Tucker guessed that this was the source of those tiny little pieces of gold that he had picked up from the stream bed.

One thing Tucker knew for sure and that was that not a living soul must know about this place until he had a chance to secure the wealth it contained. For now, he would limit his attentions to the stream outside and see how much he could get from there. Dealing with this place would take a lot of careful thought. He cast his eyes once more around the dazzling sight and then headed back to the mouth of the sinkhole.

An idea had been simmering and fermenting in Stone's mind, ever since he had found his victim absent. Why not kill another of those no-count little sodbusters? The more that he turned this thought over, the more attractive it seemed to Stone. He mounted up and then set off, back towards Indian Bluff.

When he emerged from the entrance of the cave, Tucker saw at once that a rider was moving away from his wagon. This was decidedly odd; whatever could anybody be paying a social call for at this hour of the night? He watched the horse moving and recognized its gait. It had been ridden earlier that day by the younger of the two men who had called upon him, the man who called himself Stone. This was another of Bill Tucker's talents and one which seldom was any use to him; the ability to identify most any horse at a glance. Once he had seen a mount, Tucker could generally be relied upon to pick it out again. This skill had from time to time come in handy during the war, but it was some years since he had found it of any use in civilian life. He would take oath upon it — that mean looking man had been sniffing round his belongings in the dead of night. What for was another matter entirely.

* * *

The next day, Tucker was up bright and early. He had mastered the knack of ploughing in this stony soil and managed to produce a few cables that might provide enough turfs for him to finish his house. He was building up the walls when Logan rode by. Tucker hoped that his neighbour was not about to reopen the subject of helping with the prospecting on his land, but it appeared that he wanted to talk of quite another matter. 'Andy Fisher was killed last night,' he said. 'Found outside in the fields, with his throat cut.'

'Would that be the fellow you brought here yesterday?' asked Tucker.

'Yes, yes,' said Logan impatiently, thinking how slow-witted Bill Tucker was and how unfair it should be that gold had turned up on his land. 'His wife's plumb distracted with grief.'

'I dare say,' said Tucker. 'Is there anyone suspected?'

'Well, you can guess. Leastways, most of us can.'

'Well I can't,' declared Tucker. 'Who you talking of?'

'Those bastards over at the Double D, of course. Arkwright and his boys.'

'Septimus Arkwright, would that be?' asked Tucker.

'That's right. He's got a fellow works with him, mean as all-get-out-and-push.'

'Would that be Stone?' ventured Tucker cautiously.

'That's the one. Say, d'you know him?'

'Not exactly. What time would this have been?'

'Late,' said Logan. 'Maybe one or two in the morning. Why?'

'No real reason, Just 'ravelling a thread.'

Tom Logan stared curiously at his slow-speaking and apparently slow-thinking neighbour and said, 'I mind there's more to you than meets the eye.'

Tucker shrugged. 'I guess you could say that of most folks.'

After Logan had lit out to spread the bad news, Tucker carried on building his home. While he did so, he thought carefully about the events of the last couple of days. Some of these were plain enough; Tom Logan and Andy Fisher trying to pressure him into sharing the gold, for instance. You didn't need to be any great shakes in the brains department to fathom that one out. Arkwright and Stone, now; that was a harder knot to unravel. Why had they come by his place yesterday morning and, more to the point, what was that man Stone doing, sniffing around here in the middle of the night when in the normal way of things he, Tucker, would have been sound asleep? That was a real poser!

Bill Tucker's grandma had never let anybody say in her hearing that her grandson was slow. 'The boy ain't slow,' she would say. 'He's thorough, is all.' And thorough was just precisely what Tucker was that morning, as he heaved the blocks of turf up as high as his head to complete the walls of his soddie. By the time the last piece was in position, he knew the answer to the puzzle. The man called Stone had come by last night with the intention of killing him.

When he couldn't lay hands on Bill Tucker, he had gone off and murdered somebody else.

Tucker was quite sure that he had worked out the correct answer to the perplexing sequence of events, but why anybody should want to kill him last night was quite beyond him. He supposed at first that it might be because Arkwright and Stone wanted the gold he had found, but that didn't explain why Stone had then gone straight off and killed somebody else. That made no sense at all; Andy Fisher didn't have any gold on his land. If he had done, then he probably wouldn't have been so all-fired keen on getting a share of Tucker's. No, there was no doubt that this was a regular mystery and he would need to get some more information before he was likely to be able to solve it.

★ ★ ★

Over at the Double D, Arkwright was not best pleased with his foreman.

'What in the hell ails you, Jed? What for did you kill some man whose name you don't even know? Where's the sense in it?'

Stone shrugged. 'We wanted to put fear in 'em, I don't see it makes any odds if it was Tucker or some other squatter. They'll get the message just the same.'

Septimus Arkwright mulled this over, before conceding that his foreman might have a point there. 'Mind,' he said, 'we're still no closer to getting the gold on Tucker's land. If that mortgage isn't paid off on time, it won't matter a damn how scared those men are. They'll have more than us, because at least they'll still have title to a hundred and sixty acres apiece. We won't have shit. The bank'll take the lot.'

★ ★ ★

There were two things that Bill Tucker aimed to do that day. The one was to pan a little more in the stream and the other was to take a trip into Jubilee Falls and see if Halliday wanted to buy the rest of the gold he had recently found. He needed some black powder as well and come to think of it, if folk were going to be creeping round in the middle of the night, a gun wouldn't come amiss either.

As he scooped up platefuls of sand and grit from the stream, Tucker thought of that marvellous cave that he had discovered. There looked to him to be pounds and pounds of gold embedded in the roof of that tunnel. The question was how to remove it from the rock face. He supposed that it might be possible to set a ladder up there and chip away with a hammer, but that would make for slow work. It would be easier to fix a charge there and break open the rock. The way it was positioned, all the gold and rock would then just fall down and he could sort through it at his leisure.

He was so busy dreaming about the vast quantities of gold which would be his in the future, that Tucker almost missed the nugget which was right there in front of his eyes. He damn near tipped it back in the water with the stones, absent-mindedly. It was as big as a marble and hefting it in his hand, Tucker guessed that it weighed in at over an ounce. What would that be worth? Twenty dollars?

He decided to call a halt to his prospecting for the day and go to town to talk things over with some of those who lived there. Somebody would be able to fill him in on the details of just why Septimus Arkwright and his man would be wanting to kill him or Andy Fisher. He supposed that Tom Logan must know, but somehow Tucker did not feel inclined to involve that individual in his affairs.

Mr Halliday was pleased to see Bill Tucker back at his store and he almost gasped out loud when he set eyes upon the nugget which Tucker put down on the counter so casually. It weighed in at an ounce and a half. Wait 'till he told folk in the Star of the West about this. There had been some excitement at the news of the finding of gold out by Indian Bluff, but if Carl Halliday knew anything about it, this latest find would ratchet up the interest to fever pitch. People in Jubilee Falls would be asking themselves if this was going to turn into one of those gold rush towns that you heard tell of, like Diamond City up in Montana.

Needless to say, Halliday was cheating Tucker as brazenly as he dared, figuring that there probably wasn't anybody else within a ten-mile radius who would have the wherewithal to test gold and the ready cash available to buy it. It was definitely what you might call a buyer's market and as long as he didn't overdo it, Halliday reckoned that he could pay Bill Tucker maybe two thirds or perhaps three quarters of what his finds were really worth. He underestimated Tucker's naivety though, because that individual knew very well that the scales in Halliday's store were likely to be rigged and he would be getting a lot less than his gold was actually valued at. That was what the world was like. He would have to make up the value by extracting information from the storekeeper.

'Tell me now,' said Tucker, 'I'm new to these parts, as you know. Why don't Arkwright and his man Stone take to us homesteaders?'

'Boy, you're surely as fresh and green as they come,' replied the old man with a chuckle, not at all displeased at being given the chance to explain the setup to this not overly bright specimen. 'You and the others is in Arkwright's way. 'Fore you come here, he had all that grassland and water to his self. Now you're all blocking access to water and throwing up fences and I don't know what-all else. You can see where it gets his goat.'

'So he wants us to leave, is that the score?'

'Hooeey! Are you for real?' said Halliday. ''Course he wants you to leave. He'll go bust if things carry on like this.

More people arriving every week, it's ruination to men like Arkwright, running big herds.'

Bill Tucker scratched his head thoughtfully. 'Tell you the truth, I hadn't thought of it like that. I'm much obliged to you for both the information and the twenty-two dollars.'

After leaving Halliday's store, Tucker felt that he'd better get himself equipped for trouble. Gauged by what Tom Logan and Carl Halliday had both said, his guess had been right and the foreman from the Double D had visited him the previous night with the express intention of murdering him in his sleep. This was a sobering thought and much as he disliked violence, Bill Tucker knew in his heart that if he was fixing to stay on that patch of land, then he needed to arm himself.

Halliday's store sold the kind of things you might want for inside a home, but there was another store, just across the street, which provided agricultural equipment; tools and suchlike. It also sold guns, powder and shot. The proprietor of this concern was a taciturn, dour and uncommunicative Scot called McAllister. If this man had a Christian name, then he had never shared it with the citizens of Jubilee Falls. He allowed his intimate friends, who were few and far between, to call him 'Mac'.

When Bill Tucker entered McAllister's shop, the owner swiftly dismissed him in his own mind as being just another of those little men grubbing out a wretched living by trying to grow crops out on what he thought of, remembering the Scottish lowlands of his youth, as 'the moors'. Even so, he had been raised to regard any customer as being worthy of respect and courtesy, so he greeted the man, saying, 'A vairy, vairy good day t'ye. How can I be helping ye?'

'I'd like to buy a gun please,' said Tucker hesitantly. 'A handgun.'

'Weeel, ye come to the right shop and no mistake,' said McAllister. 'Any particular sort o' weapon in mind?'

'Would you be havin' such a thing as a Navy Colt?'

'We have, although we've got more modern guns than that.'

Tucker looked apologetic, as though he might be causing some offence by his choice. He said, 'Well now, if it's no trouble, I like to stick with what I'm used to.'

This confirmed what McAllister had already decided, that here was another small-time farmer who wanted to show off by carrying a pistol on his hip. He fetched out an old Navy Colt from a cabinet behind the counter and handed it to the customer. 'Here ye are. This is what you're wanting.'

To the storekeeper's surprise, Tucker took the pistol and then examined it carefully. Then, without so much as a by-your-leave he picked up a trowel lying on the counter and used it to tap out the wedge holding the barrel in place. Having done this, he tilted the weapon so that the cylinder slipped from its spindle. He then placed the barrel and hilts of the pistol carefully down on the counter and gave his full attention to the cylinder.

McAllister watched this performance curiously, realizing that he had misjudged the man; here was somebody who knew about firearms. His customer rolled the Colt's cylinder back and forth between his palms, frowning as he did so, as if something was not quite to his liking. Then he set the cylinder down on the counter and set it slowly rolling there. He looked up and said regretfully, 'I'm sorry, but this is no good.'

'No good?' asked McAllister pugnaciously. 'Why? What's wrong with it?'

'Oh,' said Tucker, a little embarrassed, 'there's nothing wrong with it. I'm sure it'll answer for everyday use, but it wouldn't suit me.' McAllister stared at him in a way that made him feel uncomfortable, so Tucker continued reluctantly. 'See now, this cylinder is biased. If you roll it so, you can see that this side is just a shade heavier than that. Means it won't spin smooth. Look, I'll show you.' His deft hands slipped the cylinder back on to the spindle and then fitted back the barrel and inserted the wedge to secure it. Then he spun it, while holding the hammer back to let it run free. 'See,' he said. 'It'll always stop with that chamber facing down.'

The storekeeper was looking at him with an inscrutable expression on his face. 'Anything else?' he enquired ironically.

'The trigger action is stiff. Spring needs adjusting. If we take a look along the barrel, I'm guessing we'll find . . . ' As he spoke, Tucker's fingers were nimbly dismantling the pistol again. He held the barrel up to the light from the window and nodded. 'Just as I thought. Look here, the lands are burred.' He handed the barrel to McAllister, saying, 'You mind what I mean by lands, the raised parts of the rifling. Any ball from this gun will be wiggling around crooked before it even leaves the barrel.'

McAllister peered down the barrel, but it looked to him just like every other gun barrel he had ever seen. He said, 'You seem to know a deal about guns.'

'Well, I was an armourer for four years. During the war, you know. In the army.'

'I've a few other Navy Colts out the back of the shop. Will ye step through with me?' It was rare that McAllister met anybody who actually knew about firearms and there was something about this man's diffidence, almost shyness, which appealed to him. He wasn't a great one himself for pointless talk or bragging and perhaps he glimpsed a kindred spirit in this quiet individual.

In the room behind the counter, one wall was covered with shelves, several of which were loaded with various pistols. McAllister said, 'Och, I should really be lockin' these away, but all the fuss of keys and so on, I canna be bothered.' He looked through the pistols and selected one. 'Here now, this is the same model, but maybe it's in better shape.' He handed it to Tucker.

Instead of the plain, silvery steel of the standard issue Navy 0.36, this one was such a dark blue that it looked black in the dim light of the backroom. Tucker carried it out into the front of the shop and examined it by the window. Then he went through the same performance of taking the thing to pieces and testing the cylinder. He smiled approvingly and then squinted down the barrel. At last he said, 'Yes, this will do just fine. You sell powder and caps, too?'

'Aye,' said McAllister. 'That I do. You'll be wanting a holster too, I dinna doubt?'

'Oh no. Thanks anyway, but I like to have my piece near to hand, just tucked in my belt.'

When he left McAllister's store, Bill Tucker looked a different man. It was nothing you could put your finger on, but he had less of a hangdog expression on his face and there was a spring to his step. Before, had you chanced to meet him on the sidewalk, you could be pretty sure that he would move aside for most anybody. Looking at him now with that deadly weapon nestling carelessly in his belt, you might not be so confident. He looked like a man that you might not want to get crosswise to, unless you were looking for trouble.

4

When he set off back to his almost completed soddie, Bill Tucker had in his knapsack enough powder, caps, balls and shot to keep him going for a good long while. He liked the feel of the pistol against his belly as he walked; it was reassuring. Not that he hoped or expected to have to use it, it was just that after that fellow Stone had been prowling about the previous night and hearing of the murder which took place shortly afterwards, it seemed like a prudent precaution.

Handy as he was with guns and explosives, Tucker did not like violence. He had killed men during the war, in the heat of battle, but had felt bad about it afterwards. He would sooner back down and let others shoulder him to one side than fight. Just lately though, since moving to his patch of land in the shadow of Indian Bluff,

Tucker had been doing some thinking and he was coming to the conclusion that this might be the time to stop letting other people shove him around.

It had started with Logan and his friend Andy Fisher trying to force their way into a share of the gold on his land. Then with Arwright's foreman prowling round, probably with the aim of killing him, his resolve had hardened. Enough was enough. He had come out west like this and taken a quarter section of barren land, half of which was taken up by that blasted lump of rock and even then, people could not let him alone. There were still those who wanted to keep pushing him, hoping to deprive him of even that. No, it wouldn't do. It was time to let folk round here know that they had best leave him be and not trouble him further.

* * *

Earlier that day, Septimus Arkwright had summoned two of his hands and said to them, 'I want you boys to go on up to Indian Bluff and collect some rock samples for me.' Stone had told him that as a consequence of his prospecting days up in Montana, he was able to recognize gold bearing rock when he saw it. Arkwright thought that the easiest thing would be just to get a few pieces from where that fool Tucker was camped out and see what Jed Stone made of it.

'Beggin' your pardon, Mr Arkwright,' said one of the cowhands, 'but ain't that bluff been homesteaded now?'

'What of it?' replied Arkwright irritably. 'You only need fetch me a few stones from it. I'm not asking you to steal the whole damned thing.'

'Any special stones?' asked the other of the two men.

'Get me a selection. As many different kinds as you can see up there. Particularly anything with any sign of being shiny or having metal in it. Is that clear enough?'

'I guess . . . ' said one of the cowboys doubtfully.

This provoked Arkwright to say, 'You better do more than guess, boy. You want to carry on working for me? Out with it now, because if you don't, there's others as will take your bunk.'

This was enough to frighten the men into compliance. They did not wish to be thrown off the Double D, just for the sake of a few old rocks.

★ ★ ★

When he got back to his almost finished dwelling house, Tucker thought it time to see about setting the roof on the place. He had a beam of wood and some rolls of tar paper for this purpose initially, which would be sufficient to keep off showers of rain. He was unloading these from the wagon, when a movement caught his eye up on the bluff. He shaded his eyes with his hand and saw that two men were up on the rocky slopes. Watching them, he had the impression that they were looking for something that they might have dropped. The pair of them were walking about, looking at the ground and from time to time picking things up. Whatever they were doing, thought Tucker to himself, they had no business on his land. He began walking up towards the bluff to see what was going on.

Like most of the men from the Double D, the boys collecting the rocks for Arkwright didn't take the sod-busters too seriously. Sure, they were a nuisance, but there was something a little pathetic about the attempts of those poor souls who were trying to wrest a living from the grasslands. They worked all the hours God sent and never seemed to have anything much to show for it. Riding the range was a man's job, not grubbing round in mud to plant corn which would like as not fail to sprout the next year. So it was that when Tucker approached the two of them, neither man was in the least perturbed. Knowing what they did of those types, this man would most likely run off in fear if they so much as clapped their hands loud.

It was true that Bill Tucker didn't cut a very impressive figure. He was panting a little from the exertion of climbing up the slope and his face had the look of a man who was always eager to please and worried about what other folks might say or do. The cowboys nodded in a friendly enough way and carried on searching for different kinds of rocks.

'You men mind telling me what you're up to here?' asked Tucker politely.

'Just getting a few stones, is all,' said one of them. 'Nothing to fret about.'

Being spoken to in such a casual and dismissive fashion was not at all what Tucker was wanting to hear right then. He said quietly, 'Happen you don't know it, but this here is my property. You are, as they say, trespassing.'

'Well, we won't be here above another few minutes an' then we'll be off.'

The two cowboys were standing at

the foot of a sandstone cliff, which reared fifty feet above them. They had been rummaging around in the scree at the bottom of this cliff. Neither had stopped what he was doing or even bothered to turn and face Tucker properly in a civil way. It was plain that something would be needed to gain their attention. He hadn't done such a thing since the war ended, but in his defence, it has to be said that Bill Tucker was getting mighty ticked off with the way that people had been behaving since he fetched up here. In one smooth, flowing action, he drew the pistol from his belt, cocked it with his thumb, brought it up and fired twice at the rock face.

The shots sounded deafening at such proximity and the two young men, neither of whom was above twenty years of age, jerked upright in sudden fear. A chip of rock had flown from where one of the balls had struck and cut open the cheek of one of the boys. He raised a hand to it wonderingly, the realization slowly dawning that he and his partner might be in danger.

Tucker said, 'Just 'cause a man speaks politely, that's no good reason to ignore what he's a sayin'. That's just plain bad manners.'

'Sorry,' stammered one of the boys. 'We didn't mean no harm.'

'Well there's none done,' said Tucker amiably. 'You just empty out all those rocks you been pickin' up and we'll say no more about it.'

'Well, but our boss asked us most particular to bring him these.' He stopped speaking and marked where the man's pistol was aiming straight at them. With no more ado, he emptied his bag in a cascade of pebbles, rocks and stones. His companion did likewise.

'Now shake them out, so that any dust and grit come out too,' said Tucker remorselessly. 'Every last particle.'

When he was sure that the bags were quite empty, Tucker said, 'I guess your boss would be Septimus Arkwright, that so?' The boys nodded. 'Well now you can't take my rocks, but I'll give you something else to take back to your boss instead. It's a message. Think you can remember it? Here it is. Anybody takes any more stones from my property, I'm like to get pretty riled up about it. Hell, what am I saying? Stones? Anyone takes one single grain of sand from here without my say-so and I am going to take it amiss. Think you can remember to tell Arkwright that?'

The cowboys nodded and, noticing the streak of blood on the face of one of them, Tucker added solicitously, 'I'm sorry about your cheek. Comes o' not listening when a body's talking to you. Off you go now.'

After the men had left, Tucker walked back down to his soddie, feeling dissatisfied with the way that he had conducted himself. Had it really been necessary to frighten those fellows so badly? They were not really to blame for what was happening here; that was to be laid at the door of their boss. Still and all, he hadn't harmed them and maybe they would carry his message to Arkwright and that fellow would think it best to leave him be in the future. All in all, he didn't perhaps have too much to reproach himself with.

Fixing the roof beam to the top walls of the soddie was not an arduous task and neither was unrolling the tarred paper and tacking it down. Later, he would cover this temporary covering with sods of earth, which would provide insulation in the winter, but this would do for now. When he had finished, Tucker went off a few paces and then turned to admire his new home. It wasn't much to look at, but it was his own work and erected on land which belonged entirely to him. There was a satisfaction about this little achievement, building his own home, on his own land.

* * *

The two cowboys who had been driven off Indian Bluff with their tails between their legs didn't want to report in person to Arkwright and so as soon as they arrived back at the Double D, they sought out their foreman, hoping that he would be able to sooth the great man's anger when he learned of the complete failure of their expedition. Fact was, Jed Stone was every bit as contemptuous when he heard their tale as Arkwright would have been. 'You let yourself be run off the bluff by that sack o' shit? What's the matter with you boys? Strikes me you're too soft for this outfit. If that mealy mouthed little sodbuster can best you, what'll chance if you come up against a real tough challenge?'

The men wondered if they were about to be thrown off the ranch, but after thinking for a few seconds, Stone just said, 'Ah, get out o' my sight. The pair of you make me sick to look at!'

Arkwright listened carefully when this story was relayed to him by the foreman. He said, 'Sooner we get that bastard out of the way, the better. That kind of thing is catching. One day, you get one person throwing his weight round like that, next thing you know, a whole gang of men are armed and fighting off intruders.'

'I don't think we should take him at once,' said Stone. 'After last night, those farmers are goin' to be prepared for trouble. There's going to be a heap o' itchy trigger fingers out there tonight.'

'You getting scared as well?' asked Arkwright.

'No, I ain't scared. Leastways, not of any of them types. But there's no point in stirring up mischief, 'less we have good odds of coming out on top, if you take my meaning.'

Arkwright didn't say anything more for a spell, just stared out across the ranch. Then he spoke again. 'Time's running out, Jed. It's running out fast.'

* * *

Not having a horse of his own was something of an inconvenience out here and Tucker was wondering how soon he would be able to set that right. He didn't have a heap of money, but figured that if he could come up with a little more gold, that might be enough to buy a little pony. He had two aims that day. One was to do a little panning for gold and the other was to walk over and speak to one or two of the other men settled round here. He was not one to push himself forward, quite the opposite, but somebody needed to sort this mess out. It had been Andy Fisher last night, but it could be any of them next. It would be, to say the least of it, unfortunate if the other homesteaders got spooked and dug up and left. He surely didn't fancy being the only one round here to face up to Arkwright and his men.

There was something restful about scooping up the mud and silt in the old plate and watching it be carried away by the flow of the water. The first lot that Tucker collected just left a few stones behind. He tossed these on to the bank, figuring that the fewer stones there were around, the easier it would be to find pieces of precious metal. The second plate came up trumps at once. Even before all the sand had been swirled off, Tucker could see that there was a very large nugget among the stones, as well as a couple of smaller lumps.

Something which did take Tucker as being a little odd, and this only struck him at that moment, was that every single piece of gold appeared to be concentrated in a small area of the stream. Move only a short way from the old tree trunk which lay across the bank and the chances of picking anything up fell dramatically. He marked this mentally as something to investigate further, but for now, he wanted to focus upon getting all the gold out of that stream that he could. What matter if it all appeared to be in one spot? After all, there was plenty and to spare up in that cave that he had scouted last night. Enough, he calculated, to make him a rich man.

★ ★ ★

Septimus Arkwright was not a man used to making compromises. Howsoever he had his tail in a crack and was ready to settle for anything at all which would free him from this present trap. He was inclined to agree with Stone that another killing twenty-four hours after the first murder might prove counter-productive and after hearing about his two boys being run off the bluff, it seemed to him that some accommodation might have to be reached with that whoreson Tucker. He spoke briefly of his scheme to Jed Stone. 'Listen up, now. Tucker knows for a bet that we are sniffing round, hoping to get ahold of his gold. I am going to level with him.'

The thought of his boss levelling with anybody on Earth was a novel one to

Stone, but he said nothing and waited to see what would come next.

'Thing is, Jed, we need that money as desperate as can be. I don't need to tell you that. Left to his self, that little fellow won't be able to do much in the way of excavating, so why don't we offer him our help?'

'Go on,' said Stone, intrigued, 'I never had you pegged for a Christian. This talk of offering help to your neighbours shows me a new side to you.'

'Don't try and make game of me,' said Arkwright, 'I won't have it. This is what I will do. I will suggest to Tucker that we join forces. I will engage to supply as many men as necessary to dig and pan and that way, we can clear that stream of gold in no time, or at least in a good deal less than three weeks.'

'How'll that help us? I don't get it.'

'You are slow as molasses in January sometimes. Once we have fifty men working on that little stream, Tucker won't be able to see what every one of them is about. Maybe we can steal enough, without him knowing it. You know what I mean, just declaring to him enough to make it look like we're being open.'

Jed Stone considered this idea and then shook his head. 'What if he spots what you're up to and orders you and the boys off his land?'

'Then we'll bind him hand and foot and see how fast we can get a hundred and fifty ounces of gold from there. Afterwards, it will just look like a dispute between two men in partnership, nobody in town will be interested or want to take sides.'

Stone said nothing. He was starting to think that his boss was losing his grip a little, because this plan had more holes in it than a sieve. It might be worth trying, but Jed Stone was going to make plans of his own and feather his own nest, so that if it all fell apart here, he would at least have a little stake of money to get him started elsewhere.

Tom Logan was cleaning his plough when Tucker fetched up. There was something different about the fellow and it took Tom Logan a while to spot what it might be. Then it clicked; Bill Tucker was carrying. Most men hereabouts, you could tell at once when they were heeled, because they had holsters flapping against their thighs. Tucker though, he just had a pistol stuck casually in his belt, like it was the most natural thing in the world. That was another thing. Men with guns in holsters often had a look about them of: 'What a fine, dangerous fellow I am; better not fool with me, if you know what's good for you.' Logan felt that way himself when he went into town heeled on a Saturday night. There was nothing of the sort with Tucker though. He looked like he didn't much care if anybody saw that pistol there in his belt. He seemed to set no more mind to it than if it had been a pair of shears or a hammer; just another tool.

'Hidy there,' said Logan. 'What brings you out here?'

'I'm wondering what's happening 'bout that poor fellow Fisher. When will the funeral be?'

'Someone's gettin' that all fixed up with a preacher from town,' said Logan. 'His wife wants him buried on his own land.'

'Anybody in town lookin' to investigate the matter? Find out who did it?'

Logan spat a stream of tobacco juice. 'Wouldn't o' thought so. That vigilance committee of theirs is only concerned with things as happens in Jubilee Falls itself. All us out here can go hang.'

'Yeah,' said Tucker. 'That's about how I thought it'd be.'

'Did you now?'

'I guess there's no doubt in your mind that it was somebody from the Double D as did this?'

'Not the least. Why?'

Tucker formed the distinct impression that Tom Logan was being contrary and contentious. He wondered if it had anything to do with the way that he had refused to take up the offer of help from him and Andy Fisher. Well, that couldn't be helped. He said, 'I'm thinking, Logan, that we need to stand together in a business like this. Else Arkwright and his boys will chisel away at us one by one. There's strength in numbers.'

Logan turned and stared at him, like he didn't know what to say next and so Tucker went on. 'I ain't a one to put myself forward, not nohow. Still and all, something must be done.'

'And you're the one to do it, is that how the case stands?'

Tucker shrugged and Logan found the gesture irritating. 'Like I say,' said Tucker. 'I ain't a one to push to the head of the line. Someone needs to act.'

'You're somethin' else again, you know that? You ain't been here above five minutes and already you're digging a gold mine and making a name for yourself. Now you're fixing to lead us all in some kind of range war. Don't think it for a moment, Tucker. Just don't think it. You're nobody special.'

Bill Tucker gazed sadly at the blustering man in front of him. He said, 'I notice many times over the years how being scared makes some folk get agitated. I reckon you are one of that brand.' He turned and walked away, leaving Tom Logan spluttering and inarticulate with rage.

He didn't feel inclined to walk into town and see how much Halliday would give him for this latest big nugget of his. Besides which, he was already thinking that he would have to find another buyer for his gold, now that there appeared to be a regular supply of the stuff. Tucker didn't mind being cheated once in a while, but he was averse to making a habit of it. He suspected that the more he took to Carl Halliday, the more that fellow would be trying to chisel him.

It was a problem. He had no illusions at all about the likely course of events were he to go gadding off to South Pass City or somewhere a few days' travel from here. His land would be invaded in no time by various jackals and vultures, all wanting to pick over his claim. And Tucker thought that he knew who would be first in line for this thievery and that was the owner of the Double D, that man Arkwright.

They say that if you call on the Devil, he is sure to appear and although Bill Tucker was not a superstitious man, he found it slightly unnerving that no sooner had he brought Septimus Arkwright to mind, than there was the genuine article, the man himself, standing patiently by Tucker's soddie, evidently awaiting his return.

5

Arkwright smiled as soon as he caught sight of Bill Tucker coming towards him. He called out. 'A very good day to you, Mr Tucker. I just dropped by to talk a little business. Hope you're not too busy?'

This was just precisely the sort of situation that Tucker disliked. This man would engage him in a lot of talk, using a heap of long words, until Tucker didn't know if he was coming or going. Complicated debate had never been his strong point and if once he allowed Arkwright to start talking, Tucker knew that he would be lost. The only answer was to set the matter out plainly without any guile or fancy words. So he said nothing until he was a few feet from the man and then, after the usual civilities, he said, 'Mr Arkwright, I mind that you are as busy as I am. We both got work to do and neither of us want to waste our time.'

Septimus Arkwright flashed him a bright, friendly and insincere smile, saying, 'A man after my own heart. You like to get right to the point straight away. I admire that in a man.'

'Why don't we just cut to the bone at once?' said Tucker quietly and then, with a touch of embarrassment in his voice, added, 'You are wanting to steal my gold. You tried to set your man to killing me, but that didn't work and now you are going to put forward some scheme which'll tend to the same end. It won't answer.'

It was by no means a common occurrence for the owner of the Double D to be utterly lost for words, but this was one such occasion. He had seldom heard some crooked plan of his set out so neatly and accurately and it crossed his mind that he had been mistaken about this fellow. He was nobody's fool.

'Well now,' said Arkwright. 'I don't rightly know what to say. You have taken the wind right out of my sails, so to speak.' He knew that he was babbling, but really didn't know what to say next.

Tucker relieved him of the need to say anything further by saying, still in that quiet and pleasant voice of his: 'I reckon that if you just stick to your land, Mr Arkwright and leave these little homesteads alone, then there need be no trouble. You must mark well what I say 'bout my own place, too. If anybody comes on to my land without my say-so, I'm goin' to think that they are after stealing from me. I won't have it.'

Tucker's words felt like somebody had dashed a bucket of icy cold water over his head. His whole life, his very home and land, depended upon getting hold of that three thousand dollars in the next few weeks and Arkwright had really persuaded himself that he could talk around this simpleton and lay the grounds for fleecing him. To have his schemes spoken out loud by the supposed victim and to be warned off them in that blunt way was intolerable. He couldn't give up though; too much was riding on this. He would bluff.

'Mr Tucker, Mr Tucker, you got me all wrong. Nothing was further from my mind than to ride roughshod over you. I come here to offer my help.'

Bill Tucker's innate shyness and desire to please others struggled with his sense of the ridiculous and lost the battle. He laughed out loud. 'The number o' people wanting to help me since I struck gold here is purely amazing! First the other settlers and now the big ranch owner. I am beginning to feel like some kind of charity case, all the folk wanting to help me out.'

It was crystal clear that he was not going to get any change out of Tucker and so there was no point in hanging round further. There didn't seem much purpose in being polite any more either and so Arkwright vented his frustration by snarling, 'Ah, screw you!' before mounting his horse and cantering off towards the bluff.

After the ranch owner had gone, Tucker just stood there for a while, shaking his head in disbelief. When he had signed up for his quarter section, Tucker had somehow thought that he would be moving somewhere peaceful and quiet, where he would no longer be exposed to unpleasantness and bullying. It only went to show how wrong you could be.

It seemed to Bill Tucker that he needed to take counsel with others. Fisher was dead and Logan was not amenable to talking matters over in an agreeable fashion and so he would have to scout out the men in the other direction. Tucker set off on foot, with no idea of the reaction he would encounter from other settlers.

The first place Tucker came to was a neat little house, built like his own of turfs but considerably larger. There were real glass windows, unlike the open slits which served that function in the little structure he had recently thrown up. All in all, it looked like the home of somebody who takes care of things and likes to do a good job. In a narrow bed at the front of the house were a row of scarlet flowers.

As Tucker approached the soddie, a man emerged from it. He was carrying a scattergun and his expression was not a welcoming one. He called out, 'Who are you and what do you want?'

'My name's Bill Tucker. I live over yonder, by the bluff.'

'Well, that's who you are. Leastways, it's who you say you are. What d'you want?'

'You mind lowering that gun?' asked Tucker. 'I don't fancy endin' the day having to dig a charge of buckshot out o' myself.'

'Don't you fret 'bout that. I ain't never shot anything yet as I weren't aiming at.'

Nevertheless, the man, who looked to be about the same age as Tucker himself, lowered his weapon and invited his visitor to walk forward. When once the two of them were standing perhaps ten feet apart, the man said, 'Well, what brings you here?'

It seemed to Tucker that once more, this was a time for plain speaking. He said, 'A man was killed near here just a little while ago. Name of Andy Fisher.'

'I heard.'

'I was thinking that if we're wanting to avoid anything similar happening again, we should take steps to protect ourselves.'

The man stared at him for a second and then said, 'Come inside.'

The inside of the house was as neat and well-kept as the outside. A woman was sitting at a battered but clean table and she rose when the two men entered. 'Well Zac,' she said, 'not some marauder?'

'Nothing of the sort,' replied her husband. 'A neighbour. Wants to take to arms and form a militia.'

Tucker could not help but smile at this. 'Not so, ma'am,' he assured the woman. 'Only thinking about our safety.'

'Well, you men had better set down and talk. I got work to do on my vegetables.'

When they were alone, Tucker said, 'I was really only thinkin' of setting watch at night, to keep an eye out in case there is any more mischief. Nothing more.'

'You handy with that gun of your'n?' asked the man called Zac.

'Middlin' to fair,' replied Tucker modestly. 'I generally hit what I want to hit.'

'Tell you what. You come back in, say, three hours. I'll ride out and speak to one or two men. You in the army? During the war, I mean?'

'I was,' said Tucker, with some reluctance.

'What were you, officer? Private soldier?'

'I was an armourer.'

'Were you, by Godfrey? That sounds promising. Come back in a few hours and I might have some others here.'

As he left, Tucker sought out Zac's wife and said, 'Goodbye, ma'am. I hope we can become better acquainted, next time I come to visit.'

★ ★ ★

Back at the Double D, Arkwright was setting out his latest ideas to his foreman and they did not bode well for Bill Tucker. After prefacing his remarks with a variety of unflattering comments about Tucker, his manners, intelligence, way of conducting himself, style of speech, likely antecedents and various other incidental points, Arkwright came to the point.

'Tucker has to go and that right fast. We don't want to be seen to be mixed up in another killing so soon after that Fisher, so it seems to me that we'll need another to do it for us.'

'Pay someone, you mean?' asked Stone. 'That's a risky business. Suppose this hired gun talks later? That vigilance committee in Jubilee Falls might not be over concerned with what goes on out here, but they could take it into their heads to get involved if there was too much killing an' bloodshed. Happen one killing is enough for now.'

Septimus Arkwright smiled broadly. 'You're right, Jed my boy. Which is why we take care of that at the same time, while also coming out of the affair looking like the upholders of law and order. The whole thing'll be as neat as neat.'

'What you got in mind, boss?'

Arkwright told him and as he unfolded his plan, Stone's face relaxed and by the time the owner of the Double D had finished speaking, both men were grinning. It was foolproof and within forty-eight hours at most, Tucker's land would be opened up to exploitation and all their troubles should be over.

★   ★   ★

The stream seemed more swollen than it had been the day before. Maybe it was because it had its origins some way off in the Rockies, but Tucker couldn't help but notice that the water behaved with complete disregard for local conditions. Three days ago, it had been a niggardly dribble and now it was racing along like a mountain spring. He sat on the old log, watching the waters foaming and tumbling their way towards the bluff.

There was something about this gold panning game that was nagging away at the back of Tucker's mind. He needed to settle down and do some hard thinking about it, but the way things were going at the moment, he doubted that he would have the leisure to do so any time in the near future.

One thing which was troubling him was the way that he had apparently put Tom Logan out of countenance. Tucker wasn't too sure how he had done this, but the fellow surely was a little irritated. He wondered if he should go and notify Logan about the possible meeting over the way, but in the end, decided against it. Instead, he thought he'd have another turn at dredging the stream for gold. This time, he would move along different sections of the thing and see what came up. Surely, it wasn't in reason for every scrap of the gold to be found in just that one small location? If so, then there was somewhat of a mystery into which he must delve at some point. Bill Tucker took off his boots, rolled up the legs of his pants and waded into the icy water.

Had Tucker chosen instead of panning for gold to visit his neighbour once again that day, then he would have received a rude shock, because Tom Logan had visitors — an uncommon enough occurrence for him. Two horses were tethered outside his soddie, both of which would have been instantly recognizable to Bill Tucker. Inside the smoky and dark little shack, Septimus Arkwright and Jed Stone were making medicine with Logan. More specifically, they were showing him the chance to become wealthy and offering him security of his tenure on the hundred and sixty acres which he was cultivating.

'Things are getting out of hand,' said Arkwright, 'and that's the fact of the matter. There'll be fighting, bloodletting and I don't know what-all else soon.'

If Logan took this as a threat, he didn't respond, simply standing quietly to see what was being offered.

'There's that fellow up by the bluff,' continued Arkwright. 'He's as stubborn as a mule and ill-natured to boot. Not to mention where he's sitting on a heap of gold as we could all do with.' He glanced round the bare walls and floor of the soddie, before adding, 'I reckon you could do with a share of his good fortune yourself.'

Some men would have told Arkwright to come to the point and spell out what he was suggesting, but Tom Logan wasn't one of that brand. He had always found it better policy to sit tight and see how the wind was blowing before expressing his own views on any question. So he merely grunted non-committally and waited to see what would follow.

'Ah,' said Arkwright approvingly. 'You're a deep one and no mistake, Logan. You want for to know what I am coming after. All right, here's what. If Tucker was killed, then we, which is to say you and me, could work his land and recover that gold. Like as not, we could clean most of it out before anybody came sniffing round asking what we were about or where Tucker was or anything else. Agreed?'

'If you say so,' said Logan. 'What do you want of me?'

Arkwright decided that it was time to make his play. It was a gamble, but time was pressing hard and there was little time for delicacy. 'After that business the other night,' he said, 'meaning that unfortunate death as you have probably heard of, some evil-minded folks are associating my outfit with what happened. I have even heard the word 'murder' being bandied about, which is a damned lie.'

'Yes,' said Logan. 'I heard about Fisher.'

'The way things stand, if anything were to happen to Tucker, suspicion would fall at once upon me and my boys.'

'I can see where that might be the case,' said Logan, his voice expressionless. 'I reckon you have the case figured out right. Any more killing an' people will think for sure as you had a hand in it.'

Watching Logan carefully for signs of distrust or any tendency to reject his proposals, Septimus Arkwright went on. 'I have it in mind to take all my men into town tomorrow night. Least, except a few left to set a watch on my herds and suchlike. I will be turning a blind eye, if they wish to invite anybody from town to come and visit them; drinking buddies, sweethearts and anybody else who wants to go up to the Double D. You with me so far?'

'I reckon. You're goin' to make sure that you, him there as is your foreman and all the rest of your boys is seen by a heap of folk tomorrow night.'

'Couldn't have put it better myself. If something happens to Tucker, nobody will be able to come accusing me of assassinating him.'

'Where do I fit in?' asked Logan bluntly. 'What will you have me do?'

It was now or never and Arkwright took the plunge. 'I want you to go and kill Bill Tucker and then you can share the gold as we dig up from his land. More than that, when the rest of these fellows settled here is being swept away, I'll leave you be. You can carry on living here. What d'you say?'

For a spell, Logan said nothing and the expression on his face gave nothing away either. Just as Arkwright was beginning to think that he had made a terrible miscalculation and that the man before him would ride off to town and spread the story of what had been planned, Tom Logan stretched out his hand and said, 'What do I say? I say you got yourself a deal, Mr Arkwright.'

* * *

Starting at the first sinkhole, that from which the spring emerged, Tucker worked his way systematically along the bed; sampling the silt every twenty yards or so. There was nothing, not a single trace of gold. He returned to where the decaying tree trunk overhung the bank and then plunged his plate deep into the mud and grit. Swirling the plate from side to side, Tucker saw at once that among the stones which remained, there were two tiny fragments of gold. His brow furrowed in perplexity.

There was no doubt at all that there was a vast lode of gold, just a short way into the cave from which the stream emerged on to his land. Tucker had seen it with his own eyes. But the gold which had worn away from there was all trapped in just one small place in this stream. He wondered if the current of the water had something to do with it. What was it about that particular spot which was catching all the precious metal right there?

★　★　★

After leaving Logan's place, Septimus Arkwright and his foreman rode along for a while in companionable silence. At length, Stone observed, 'I never thought the fool would go for it so quick!'

'I know men. He's a greedy fool and his eyes are dazzled by the glitter of gold. That's as far as he can see. It's like drink with some men. Reason flies out the window.'

'You don't think he'll work out what's to do? After we've left him and he has time to think it over, I mean.'

'Not he,' said Arkwright confidently. 'All he's thinking about right this minute is how to spend all the money he's going to have. That's all as'll occupy his mind 'till tomorrow night.'

'Poor sap!'

'Like I say, I know men.'

The town of Jubilee Falls had sprung up without any planning, from a group of wooden buildings belonging to some of the earliest settlers. One or two of these old stables, sheds, barns and outhouses still remained, including one very capacious barn in the middle of town. Being right on Main Street, this structure was no longer used for its original purpose, of course. Instead, it made a convenient place for large gatherings, such as would not be able to be contained in the church or saloon. In particular, it was used for dances and Arkwright had begun spreading word that such an event could be expected the following night. All his men were told that they were either to be there and make themselves visible to the town, or they could just move on and consider themselves no longer to be in the employ of the Double D. A similar ultimatum was issued to those whose duties up at the ranch would prevent them from going to the ranch. Every man jack of them was to invite at least one person from the town to come and visit during the dance.

There was much grumbling and not a little bewilderment about these orders from the boss. In the normal way of things, Arkwright hated to see strangers hanging around his spread and more than one man had been summarily dismissed for being found canoodling in a field with some girl from the town.

'What d'you make of it?' asked one baffled cowboy in the bunkhouse that evening. 'Meaning about us all having to go to some dance?'

'Don't rightly know,' replied his friend. 'I'm on duty here in any case.'

'You bringing anybody up here?'

'You bet. You know Callie-Ann? Sweetest little trick in shoe leather you ever did see and the boss says I can have her up here as long as I care for tomorrow. Ain't that something else again?'

In order to make sure that enough

townsfolk turned up at the barn, Jed Stone had put it about that there would be a group of musicians playing the dance music, to say nothing of various other vague attractions. The rumour in town was that there might be free ale; which in itself was more than enough to guarantee a good turnout.

Stone had a lot of difficulty about the musical entertainment, on account of not having any musicians among the men on the Double D. He began to get pretty ticked off when one after the other, the cowboys claimed to have no instruments and to be quite unable to play them, even if they could be procured. He began cursing them and their families in the foulest terms, until one man owned to having a harmonica tucked away in his pack. Then, another of the men confessed that he had a fiddle, but that it lacked a string. In any case, he could not really play it, but had taken it in part payment of a gambling debt. Finally, Stone found that one man was reasonably proficient at the tin whistle, although his repertoire was exceedingly limited.

Even the dullest of the hands knew by this time that something was afoot and that the dance itself must surely be a cover for something the boss planned. Nobody said this out loud, but by means of raised eyebrows and half-smiles, they managed to convey to each other that the following night might prove pretty lively, not just for those as was going to the dance, but for somebody else somewhere. In this, they were right; although they could not have guessed the outcome of the evening.

6

The owner of the Double D was banking heavily upon none of the homesteaders hearing about his dance. It was for this reason that he had chosen to hold it at such short notice, calculating that word would not have reached people like Tucker by the time that the event actually took place. If Tom Logan were to be able to take out Tucker, then it was vital that his victim be on his land tomorrow during the dance.

In fact Bill Tucker did learn about the barn dance when he went into town to buy some provisions. His first port of call was Halliday's store, where he sold the little pieces of gold that he had not already disposed of. 'I make that a little over ten dollars I owe you,' said Halliday, wondering how much longer he would be able to cheat Tucker in this way before that individual smelt a rat. 'Can I offer you any goods for sale? A nice carriage clock, perhaps or a framed print for your wall?'

'Thanks, but no,' Tucker told him. 'I'm a mite too busy just at the minute for sitting round admiring etchings and such.'

'Will you be going to the dance tonight?'

'Dance?' said Tucker. 'What dance might this be?'

'Quite a swell affair, from all that I'm able to apprehend. Mr Arkwright up at the Double D is laying it on. I don't rightly mind for what reason.'

Even had Tucker been a one for dancing, which he was not, the very fact that Septimus Arkwright was organizing this dance would have been enough to put Tucker off going. His code of honour forbade him from accepting hospitality from a man he disliked. He thought it would have been hypocritical of him to show up at the dance. To make conversation, he asked, 'Many people expected?'

'The whole town, from what I hear,' said Halliday. 'Mr Arkwright is laying on music and there will be free drinks, leastways, from what I heard.'

'I think I'll pass on it for myself, but I dare say folk'll have fun there.'

Tucker's next stop was McAllister's store, across the way. The Scotsman was pleased to see him. As a rule, McAllister found that most of the people with whom he came into contact talked a great deal too much for his taste. His economy of words had been formed when, at his mother's knee, she had told him repeatedly, 'When ye've something tae say, then say it. An' then when ye've said it, close your mouth and stop speaking.' This approach to conversation had always served McAllister well and he was amused to come up against somebody who was even more sparing in his words than he was himself.

'Guid morning to ye,' said McAllister. 'It's Mr Tucker, is it not?'

'Why yes, that's my name. Tell me, do you sell black powder in large amounts?'

McAllister raised a quizzical eyebrow. 'Weel now, that depends how large the amount is, I suppose. What have ye in mind?'

'Could you sell me ten pounds? Fifteen would be better, but I could make do with ten.'

The storekeeper stared hard at the innocuous looking man standing before him. He said, 'I have enough to sell ye fifteen pounds, but that's an affle large quantity. It's none o' my business, but you know what ye're about with the stuff?'

'I do, yes,' said Tucker and with no more ado, McAllister went into his back room and began weighing out the powder.

★　★　★

Arkwright and Stone were putting the finishing touches to their scheme and both were feeling pretty pleased with what they were setting up. Both men had gone over the idea a dozen times, looking for flaws and drawbacks. None had become apparent and unless there was some unexpected development, then Bill Tucker's land should be wide open for the taking within less than twenty-four hours. There was just one further little detail that needed to be arranged and that was such a strange one that Stone was wondering how the men he had selected for the task would react. It was to be none other than a moonlit picnic up on Indian Bluff for two of the hands and their sweethearts from the town. This might sound like a right attractive idea, except that Jed Stone would be coming along to play gooseberry and he would be taking with him a most unusual weapon. The trap was laid, the bait in place and all that remained was to watch the prey fly into the cage.

* * *

He really would need to acquire a horse or pony, thought Tucker as he trudged home with the fifteen pound keg of powder slung on his back. There were three yards of fuse as well and he now felt ready to begin preparations for extracting the gold from his land wholesale, rather than in little dribs and drabs, the way that he had been up to now.

Nitro would have been better for his purpose, but it was not in reason that he should expect to be able to lay his hands on a supply of nitroglycerin in an out-of-the-place like this. The black powder would do; it would have to. He would, thought Tucker, have to be mighty careful about how much he used for the job. Too much and he was going to collapse the cave entirely and bury all the gold under the hillside. He wanted to use just enough to break up the rock and bring large chunks of it raining down. There would be some work needed beforehand, chiselling holes and so on into the rock face. It had been some years since he had undertaken anything like this and Tucker was relishing the challenge.

* * *

Arkwright didn't usually invite his foreman into the house, preferring to keep his relations with Stone as a business kind of thing, rather than acting like they were bosom friends. There was something about having a fellow in your home which made it harder to maintain that master and servant atmosphere which was so necessary for good order. This afternoon was different though. They had to talk things over, examine equipment and generally arrange matters in a private fashion; not under the eyes of any casual passer-by.

'Set yourself down there,' Arkwright said, indicating a sofa. 'I'll go and fetch the rifle.'

The room in which he left Stone was well furnished without being vulgar and extravagant. Everything in the room was expensive, but didn't look so at first glance. It was a far cry indeed from Stone's modest little place, up near the bunkhouses. One day, he thought, I shall have just such a room as this in which to spend the evening. Don't I deserve it just as much as the boss does? Maybe more. His reverie was interrupted by Arkwright's return.

Arkwright had in his hands a rifle of most unusual design. It looked as though somebody had taken into their heads to marry a telescope to a musket. A long, brass tube ran the whole length of the weapon's barrel, terminating level with the hammer, on the left hand side. Stone said, 'It's a while since I laid eyes on one of those and that's a fact.'

'It sights up to eight hundred yards, which is a shade under a half mile. You reckon you can shoot straight at that range?'

Jed Stone laughed out loud. 'I killed men at greater distances than that, lemme tell you.'

'You use one of these before?'

'A Whitworth? Sure. Let me hold it and remind myself of the feel of the thing.' Stone stood up and took the rifle from his boss's hands. 'Heavier than I recollect. That's good, it'll help damp down the kick.'

'Take it over to the window there and sight through the telescope. Mind nobody sees you though.'

Jed Stone carried the long weapon over to the window and then fiddled with the sights and the telescope; adjusting them both to his own satisfaction. Then he squinted down the brass tube and, while doing so, pointed the gun at the hills visible from the parlour window.

'Remember,' said Arkwright, 'You'll be resting it on a rock tonight, which will make for easier aiming. It's a muzzle loader, you know. That means you're only going to get one shot. You have to take your man first time and be sure that he's dead into the bargain. You sure you're up to the job?'

Stone turned a cold eye on the owner of the Double D. 'I've killed heaps o' men in my time. I'm up to it,' he said briefly.

'Let's run through it again,' said Arkwright.

'We been through it a dozen times.'

'Yeah, well let's make it a baker's dozen. Tell me how you'll play it.'

Like a child saying his lesson or reciting a party piece, Stone said in a bored voice, 'I go up behind Indian Bluff with Jenkins and Connelly, and their bits of skirt of course. We make out it's a romantic picnic and when we get to the top, I go off and leave them some privacy. Then when I see Logan approaching Bill Tucker's place, I draw the men's attention to it and remark that it seems strange. I will express the hope that there's no mischief afoot.'

'So far, so good. You make sure that those two boys break off whatever the hell they're up to and gaze down themselves. Make sure the girls hear the conversation. By the by, you ain't explained to them yet why you're carrying a military sniper's rifle.'

'That's the weak part. The boys'll never buy it.'

'Doesn't matter a shit if they do or they don't. They'll already know that something is going on, from you ordering them up on to the bluff for a picnic in the middle of the night.'

'All right, I'll say that I'm carrying this thing so as to ward off coyotes or wolves. Boy, it's awful thin.'

'No matter. What then?'

'I already told 'em as I'm afeared that there is trouble in the wind. We all watch quietly 'till Logan shoots Tucker down. Then I give a cry of anger or disgust, like I'm outraged at seeing such a scurvy trick being played. Go on about cowardly assassins and suchlike.'

'Yes, we'll take it as read. Then what?'

'Then, I shoot Logan through the head, making sure that he is stone dead.'

★ ★ ★

Bill Tucker was not a cunning or duplicitous man, but at the same time, he was no fool. His might not be the sharpest mind of the age, but he could see well enough that a number of people in the area were after the gold on his land. He was also aware that there was the wider question of how much longer it would be before the owner of the Double D made an attempt to drive some of the homesteaders from their land. From that perspective, he was doubly at risk. Arkwright wanted his land and gold both.

Zac Hardy had introduced him to some other men the previous evening and when it had been revealed that Tucker was an expert in firearms and explosives, the four other men treated him like his views might be worth more than their own. This was a novelty for Bill Tucker and he tried to live up to their expectations. Nobody at that meeting said so in so many words, but he had the distinct idea that the others were looking to him to provide a lead.

In the meantime, there was the matter of getting at the gold which was embedded high in the roof of the limestone cave from which the stream across his land issued forth. Now he didn't want anybody to see him entering or leaving that sinkhole, because it might provide a clue to those hoping to steal his gold. He had no idea if he was being watched, but it was probably not a bad thing to act as though he were constantly under observation from hostile elements. Tucker was itching to go back into that cave and start laying the groundwork to a spot of demolition, but he decided that it would be better done under the cloak of darkness.

* * *

In Jubilee Falls, there was a certain amount of excitement about the dance that evening. Arkwright had sent some men down to decorate the barn and they had been busy tying coloured ribbons round the doors and adding other touches suggestive of gaity. The man with the fiddle, the other with the harmonica and the boy who played the tin whistle had arrived and were trying to find a few tunes that they could all play at more or less the same time. Passers-by advanced the thesis that the noise emanating from that barn sounded like a dozen cats being roasted over a slow fire.

Jed Stone was priming Jenkins and Connelly for the possibility that there might be some unexpected action during their picnic. He took the two of them to one side and said, 'I'm coming along of the two of you and your girls, so's I can set watch for wolves and such, while you boys relax.'

An embarrassed silence followed this news. They knew as well as Stone that the chances of their being attacked by a pack of hungry wolves were about the same as the odds on Stone himself being elected President of the United States, but they had both worked at the Double D long enough to know when to shut up and keep their own counsel.

If all went smoothly, then both Tucker and Logan would be dead in a few hours. Logan would be cast in the role of the murderer of Andy Fisher and Bill Tucker, while Stone himself would be seen in the character of avenging angel — the righteous man who witnessed a brutal slaying and then reacted instinctively to end the life of the vicious assassin. There would be four witnesses to both Logan's murder of Tucker and also his own retributive killing of Tom Logan. It was as neat a double cross as Jed Stone could ever remember.

It's one thing to make complicated plans with each step of the way depending upon the one before having been perfectly executed, but where such endeavours almost invariably fall down is in their reliance upon fallible humans. When your next move relies upon three, four, five or even more ordinary people doing just precisely as you expect them to do, then something is bound to misfire. So it was that evening.

The weak link in the whole business was Tom Logan. Some people, and they are, mercifully, few and far between, are natural born killers. Jed Stone was one such man, a man who would snuff out the life of a fellow being without giving it half a second's thought. He had cut Andy Fisher's throat without any qualms at all and was quite ready to commit murder again as soon as was needed. For most folk though, taking the life of a human is a fearful and awe-inspiring prospect. When they do kill somebody, it is on the spur of the moment, when they are in a passion or liquored up. That way, they are spared from the necessity of brooding before-hand on the preparation and planning of the act.

Tom Logan had agreed to kill Tucker, but he wasn't feeling any too happy about it. The man had rubbed him up the wrong way, for which Logan could not forgive him, but that didn't mean that he wanted him dead. When he had gone over to see what poor fool had ended up with the quarter section which included Indian Bluff, Tom Logan had enjoyed commiserating with Tucker and finding a man who was in a worse case than he was himself. It was irritating to watch the philosophical way that Tucker accepted his bad fortune and then later, when he struck gold, there was a pang of jealousy and the feeling that he, Logan, had been cheated.

The last straw had come when Tucker came by his place, trying to lord it over him and set himself up as a man of consequence. This irked Logan so much that he was fit to burst and when Arkwright had put his deal forward, why then it was little wonder that Logan had snapped off his hand in his eagerness to accept it. Now, he wasn't so sure.

Like many weak men who are facing a problem, Tom Logan ducked it and instead of dealing with the thing squarely, he ran away and hid. In his case, hiding took the form of seeking refuge in a bottle of rye whiskey. There was no question of not undertaking the task which he had engaged to accomplish for Arkwright. Logan was up to his neck in debt in Jubilee Falls and unless he came up with some cash money pretty damned soon, he would have to dig up and leave. However, he had nowhere to go, having failed comprehensively in three other districts. Coming out to Wyoming as a homesteader had been the last throw of the dice for him and if he left there now, penniless and alone, then he might as well curl up in a ditch someplace and die. He needed the money from that gold every bit as badly as Septimus Arkwright.

A natural consequence of all this was that by the time the sun set on the evening of the dance, Tom Logan, although still quite determined to shoot an innocent man for the sake of his gold, was as drunk as a lord.

★ ★ ★

Nobody in town asked themselves why Arkwright should have taken it into his head to organize a dance. Diversions were few and far between in Jubilee Falls and folk were just pleased to have any sort of entertainment laid on. Septimus Arkwright made sure to appear early on and beam genially at those enjoying themselves. Inwardly, he was seething and cursing them all to hell. The rumours about free drinks had turned out to be partly true. Three casks of ale had been provided at Arkwright's own expense and the sight of all those oafs drinking his money away was annoying the owner of the Double D greatly. At least the 'band' was producing something which might have been music, always providing you had had a few drinks and were no sort of connoisseur.

The happiest group of folk that night was probably the picnickers who were making their way up the side of the bluff facing away from Tucker's soddie. The only fly in that ointment was the presence of Jed Stone, who had earlier scouted out the scene and knew just exactly where he wanted everybody when things blew up, down below. He had even chosen the very rock from which he would be taking his shot. He and the others in his party were maybe a hundred feet above the plain and roughly a quarter mile, as the crow flies, from Tucker's soddie.

Pete Jenkins and Jack Connelly didn't know any of this. They had figured right enough that there was something in the wind, which Stone hadn't seen fit to share with them, but then they weren't really fussed. As long as the hulking, surly foreman kept a distance from the two couples, looking out for wolves or whatever foolishness he was about, they could get on with a little courtship.

If Jenkins and Connelly were the happiest that evening, then the most miserable by a long sight was Tom Logan, who by the time that twilight had covered the land was in that state of stupefied intoxication where a man feels bitterly unhappy and maudlin. In a saloon, Logan would by this time be leaning too close to other patrons, breathing whiskey fumes in their faces and confiding in them how life had dealt him a succession of poor hands. As things stood, he had nobody on whose shoulder he could cry and so he checked that his gun was loaded and stumbled out of his door in search of Bill Tucker.

So far, everything was, on the face of it, going perfectly according to the plans which Arkwright and Stone had laid. If only Tom Logan could find and kill Tucker and then stand still long enough for Jed Stone to blow his head off, then the fortunes of the Double D might yet be saved.

7

It was Jed Stone who first knew that things were likely to miscarry. While the two couples were eating, drinking and chatting amiably, some twenty five yards from the rock where Stone had positioned himself, the foreman was watching Tucker's soddie. The light was almost gone and the moon visible in the sky, when he saw Bill Tucker walk out of his home and stride purposefully towards the stream which flowed across his land. He was carrying a storm lantern, which cast a flickering light around him as he walked.

Stone muttered an oath and watched in growing dismay as Tucker moved further and further from his home. This was the first intimation that things were beginning to unravel. Stone had taken some time to sight the Whitworth and line up his shot. The whole business was predicated on the assumption that he would be shooting Logan, while the man was standing outside the soddie. Stone craned his head round, just in time to see Tucker vanish into the little cave from which the stream flowed.

'What the hell is he up to?' wondered Stone out loud. Then, a movement on his left caught his attention and he saw that some drunk was staggering along, weaving unsteadily from side to side, towards Bill Tucker's soddie. At this sight, an even stronger oath escaped from Stone's lips, when he saw that it was Tom Logan. It needed no ability to foretell the future, to see that things were about to go seriously wrong.

* * *

Finding good locations to place the charges was not going to present any difficulty. The limestone of the cave was cracked and seamed all over and the water had enlarged some of these cracks over the years, until they were a foot wide. The main problem, thought Tucker, was going to be the damp. He would need to wrap the powder in oil cloth, as well as decanting it into suitable containers. It was of course also important that the fuse didn't get damp. He would make a start on the operation tomorrow night. Anybody hearing the explosion would not be likely to make anything of it. Tucker doubted that they would guess that someone was rock blasting in the area. He still didn't want to draw attention to the sinkhole, because if his activity brought down a load of rock and gold, then he really didn't wish to advertise the fact.

Up on Indian Bluff, Stone watched helplessly as Tom Logan staggered up to Tucker's soddie, shouting for him to come out and be a man. The two couples behind him could hear the shouting and were making jokes about somebody not being able to hold his liquor, by the sound of it. It was then that Stone saw the gleam of lamplight which signalled the reappearance of Bill Tucker from the sinkhole.

Tucker heard Tom Logan shouting and hollering as soon as he came out of the cave. He could tell immediately that the fellow was drunk. Then, as he listened to his shouting, Tucker realized that it was a series of threats against his life. 'I'm goin' to kill you Tucker, you son of a bitch!' shouted the inebriated man. 'You best get a ready to die now!' Although he had no idea what was to do, Tucker thought it a prudent precaution to pull the pistol from his belt and cock it. After doing so, he opened the lantern and extinguished the flame. There was no point in making himself a better target than he already was.

'What's all the hollerin'?' said Pete Jenkins, who had crept up noiselessly behind Stone.

'Just some drunk,' replied Stone casually. 'Nothing to pay heed to.'

'Who's he threatening to kill?'

'How the devil should I know?'

growled Stone. Now the other man and the two girls had abandoned their romantic assignation and were also peering down at the drama unfolding below. Connelly said, 'Hey, that's that fellow Tucker who found the gold.'

'Is it?' said Stone. 'I can't make it out from up here.' Then the shooting began.

Tucker had worked out that Tom Logan wasn't overkeen on him, but he hadn't for a moment thought that it was bad enough that the man would wish to kill him. He walked on towards where Logan was shouting threats and abuse and then, when he was a little way off, he said loudly, 'Logan, you're in no fit state. Why don't you get yourself back home and sleep it off.'

This well-meaning piece of advice infuriated the drunken man, because he turned in the direction of Tucker's voice and let fly with a shot. It missed him by a mile, but alerted Bill Tucker to the fact that this was a good bit more serious than he had thought. He considered trying to disarm the fellow, but the thought came to him that he would have to get right up close to accomplish such an end. He could easily get himself shot in the process.

'You bastard, snotnosed cowson,' shouted Logan. 'Tryin' to put yourself forward and make out you're so damned special. Well you ain't.'

'Logan,' said Tucker. 'You're apt to regret this in the morning.' Another ball whistled past him, closer than the first. As peaceable and easygoing as he was, it was dawning on Bill Tucker that if he didn't take some step, then this was going to end in his death. He tried once more. 'I got no quarrel with you. Let's just go our ways.'

This time, the ball struck the turf right between Tucker's feet; throwing up grit which struck his pants. Enough was enough. He raised his pistol, bent his left arm and held it at chin height to rest his right wrist on and then drew down on Tom Logan. Logan was staring stupidly at the ground, but then he lifted his head and raised his hand, obviously getting ready to fire again. Tucker fired one shot, which went straight through Logan's forehead, taking out some of his head as it exited messily from the back of his skull. The man was dead before he dropped to the turf.

'Holy shit,' breathed Connelly. 'Did you see that?' He turned to the foreman and said injudiciously, 'I wonder you didn't lend a hand there and shoot the one who was trying to kill Tucker. You surely got the right weapon for it.'

Jed Stone, turned to Connelly and stared at him coldly for a few seconds, before remarking, 'You got a big mouth, you know that?'

★   ★   ★

The next day, the shooting out at Indian Bluff was the talk of Jubilee Falls. The two girls had witnessed the whole thing and so there was no question of Tucker being in any sort of trouble. It was as clear-cut a case of self-defence as you could ever hope to see.

As he made preparations for blasting the cave that day, Bill Tucker thought about the shooting and wondered if he should have acted any differently. Shooting to wound was all a lot of nonsense and if he had done that, then it would have been just his luck if Logan had managed to get off another shot at him — maybe one which hit him this time. As for jumping the man and relieving him of his weapon, well that kind of thing was all well and good in a dime novel, but it wouldn't answer in real life. No, it was a sad fact that he had been left with no other choice than to kill Tom Logan.

Before going about his own business that day, Tucker had loaded the dead man on to his cart, harnessed up the ox and drawn the mortal remains of Thomas Logan back to his own land. There, he had with great reverence, lifted the corpse down and then taken it into the soddie and laid it on the bed. If others wished to dispose of it, then they would be able to do so.

There had been something shocking about the hatred in Logan's voice. Tucker simply couldn't think what he had done to drive the man to the point of murder. It was typical of Bill Tucker that he should look for the cause within himself, rather than attributing the fault to others.

★ ★ ★

Arkwright was feeling very low that morning. He had spent good money on setting up that wretched barn-dance, even provided liquor and musical entertainment and it was all simply money thrown in the mud. What his next move would be, he really didn't know. It was Stone who gave him the clue. They had talked over the way that Logan had bungled what was really a very simple and straightforward job and there looked on the face of it to be nothing to retrieve from the disaster. It was while Arkwright was rehearsing over and over in his mind what his foreman had told him that he suddenly twigged. And when he did so, he knew that he had been making things needlessly complicated and that as was so often the case, the direct route would be the simplest and best. He went in search of Jed Stone.

'What do you think Tucker was up to in that sinkhole?' asked Arkwright when he had run his foreman to earth, 'Why'd he go off there after dark?'

'Why'd most folk do stuff after dark,' replied Stone. ''Cause they don't want others to know what they're about.'

'That's the way I read it too. Tucker's got something in that cave as he doesn't want to draw attention to.'

'Like what?'

'Lordy Jed, but you can be right slow on the uptake at times. What's come out o' that hole in the ground? What're we after ourselves? What's in the blasted stream?'

'You mean gold?' said Stone. 'Yes, it could be. That placer has to come from somewhere.'

'Placer? What's that?'

'It's what we call native gold, stuff just laying around where you can pick it up. The metal that you get by panning is placer. Sometimes, you get it on the ground as well, if the lie of the rocks is right.'

'What do you say to the chance that Tucker has found the source of the gold in that stream of his, buried in the rocks in that hillside?'

The other shrugged. 'It could be so.'

'Here's one last question. We don't want any more shooting or killing for a bit, but how long would it take, you think, for anybody to miss Tucker? Like, if he just vanished. Who'd notice and how long would it be?'

Jed Stone thought this over, while rubbing his chin. 'I'd say that if any o' them squatters was to vanish, it would be weeks before anybody would ask questions. They're always going off somewhere, or just so busy working that they don't visit town. I don't rightly know. Couple o' weeks? Longer?'

'Yes,' said Septimus Arkwright. 'I was of the same mind myself.'

* ★ ★

It was hardly necessary to work with the hammer and chisel which he took into the cave that morning. Tucker wedged a stave of wood in one of the larger cracks and then hung the lamp from it. Then he worked his way round systematically, plotting out the network of seams and cracks that could take charges. One of the deepest cracks was two feet wide and went back as far as his arm could reach.

Every so often, Tucker would glance up at the ceiling and admire the twinkling of light which the tumbling water reflected from the storm lantern and up on to the reef of gold. He had toyed with the idea of erecting ladders or scaffolding here and then chipping away at the rock, but that would be a mighty time-consuming and laborious process. He wanted to get as much of that gold down as could be and then store it somewhere safe. Tucker was under no illusions at all about what would happen when he took the gold he recovered by blasting into South Pass City. A bunch of thieves would fetch up here, while he was gone, and start looting for all they were worth. Heading the line would most likely be that scoundrel Arkwright.

It took most of the morning, working under the most tiresome conditions for him to get everything just as he wanted it. Tucker aimed to set off one small charge first and then gradually work his way up to larger and larger charges, until he could bring down that section of the roof which held the gold. It would be a tricky operation, but he had little doubt of his ability to undertake the job. He had no watch, but when his stomach was beginning to rumble from hunger, Tucker decided that he should end the shift and go and get some vittles into himself.

It felt good to be in the fresh air again and under God's blue sky. Back at his soddie, Tucker found a half loaf of bread which was not yet completely stale and then carved himself a piece of cheese. It would do for the time being, washed down by some water from the stream. He was about to head back that way, when he saw a rider approaching from the opposite direction to the bluff. There was no reason to suspect trouble, but he automatically checked that the pistol in his belt was loose and ready to pull if need arose.

The man on the horse was the one called Zac. He greeted Tucker shortly and then, after dismounting and without wasting any words, said, 'Me and my neighbours, we was most favourable impressed by what you said the other night. Touching that is upon forming some sort of guard to protect our land. Most everyone expects that Arkwright to try and put the bite on us soon and kind o' ease us out of the area.'

'Which is much what I was thinking too,' said Tucker. He waited to see what would come next.

'None of us take overmuch here to bosses and folk telling us what to do. Maybe that's why some of us come out here to these new territories.'

'Well,' said Tucker slowly, 'you might have a point there. You just might. I can't say as I ever took to being bossed around myself.'

'Mind,' said Zac, 'sometimes you needs to choose one fellow to kind of lead things, if you know what I mean. Not,' he added quickly, 'as he is better than the rest. More that he is someone who knows what's what.'

'I'm sorry,' said Tucker. 'I'm a simple soul and you lost me altogether now. What have you come out here to tell me?'

'Why, that me and the others was hopin' as you'd consent to lead the way a little in resisting any attempt to drive us off our land. Seems to us that a man who knows a deal about powder and shot would be the most handy to have for such an enterprise.'

Of all the unlikely things which the man before him could have said, this was the most unexpected and surprising. It would be no exaggeration to say that Bill Tucker was stunned. It was certainly the first time in his life that anybody had asked him to lead anything. He felt that he should express his appreciation, but Zac wasn't a one for that kind of carry-on.

'If you'll do this, it'll ease my mind greatly. I think that firearms are likely to be the key here and that it will come to some hard fighting sooner or later,' Zac said.

'You want that I come over to your place tonight and we can make some plans?'

'Yes, I'll put the word out. We'll see what's best. Come by about an hour after sundown.'

★ ★ ★

Arkwright wondered if he was developing some species of obsession about Bill Tucker. The man seemed to crop up at every touch and turn. Everything that Arkwright wanted, Tucker appeared to guard the way to it. It was partly because until pretty recently, Septimus Arkwright had not been crossed for years and when you get into the custom of having your own way, you start thinking after a while that that is the natural order of things. Those who step in your way then begin to look like they are challenging the established order. That was pretty much how Arkwright was viewing the little man out by Indian Bluff.

Of one thing, Arkwright was certain. That was that Bill Tucker had an almost unlimited supply of gold on his land. The stuff must be laying round in the water and in the cave from which the stream ran. The more he thought about it, the more the owner of the Double D persuaded himself that all his troubles would be at an end if he could just lay his own hands on Tucker's supply of precious metal.

★　★　★

It was time to dig up a good amount of gold from the stream. Tucker was running a little low on supplies and could do with a little cash money. After Zac had ridden off, he picked up his spade, a zinc pail and one or two other things and then made his way to the spot by the old tree trunk where he had been most successful so far. Actually, it was not that he had been 'most successful' at that location; in truth, he had not found so much as a grain of gold at any other place.

He put down his tools by the mossy old log and took off his boots. Then Tucker climbed into the water with the pail and began scooping large amounts of mud and silt out. He tipped the pail on its side under the water, in order to let the lighter earth fall out and be carried off by the current. In this way, he could process more material than he was able to do with the old china plate.

Half an hour's work in this way yielded only three small pellets, weighing perhaps half an ounce in total. A chill dread seized Tucker; it seemed that the stream had given up as much gold as it was going to. Until he had blasted the rock face in that limestone cave, there would be no more gold to sell.

Bill Tucker spent another hour panning the stream. He even went back to the soddie for his old plate and tried that, but it was all to no avail. It made no sense at all, but from all that he was able to collect, the stream had now been worked dry.

★   ★   ★

For the second time in as many days, Septimus Arkwright had invited his foreman into the house for a conference. It was, thought Arkwright to himself, becoming a bad habit. He might as well ask Stone to move into the spare bedroom at this rate.

'Listen now, because if we don't move pretty damn fast, we are finished,' he told Stone. 'The key here is that we don't want any more killing to be seen taking place for a spell. I hear rumours that those boys in town who run the vigilance committee are saying that they should be assuming some kind of responsibility for the homesteaders as well.'

'That happens, we're done for,' Stone muttered. 'We can't fight those squatters and the town both.'

'Think I don't know that? What sort of fool do you take me for? That's why we got to do everything sharpish. Before others try to stick their nose into our affairs, you get me?'

'So what'll you have?'

'Tonight, we put the fear of God into some of them sodbusters. We get a bunch of boys to ride down, torch a few things, pull up fences maybe. No shooting anybody or aught of that sort, just enough action to leave 'em wondering what will happen next if they don't take the hint. Then, tomorrow night, we take Tucker.'

'Yeah,' said Stone, almost smirking. 'I recollect that we tried that game last night. See the result, now. Tucker still on his land and shows no sign of moving away any time soon. You think to scare him off?'

'No, he ain't the type to scare like that. I thought he was, but I was wrong. I will tell you exactly how we deal with him, but in the meantime, get some of the tougher boys rounded up and tell 'em there's a bonus paid for all who ride with us tonight. Make sure they know that there's no killing in the case, just making those dirt farmers afeared.'

★ ★ ★

Since shooting Tom Logan, Tucker hadn't really given a lot of thought to the fellow. Sure, he was puzzled as to why a man should have taken so much against him that he would come here to try and kill him, but that was all. It had been a case of kill or be killed and he didn't have a bad conscience about shooting the fellow, any more than he would about having killed a dog with rabies. It was just one of those unpleasant necessities which came up from time to time. He wondered if it was something that he should mention that evening when he went by Zac's house, but decided that it most likely didn't signify.

* * *

As evening approached, Arkwright went to speak to the five men who Jed Stone had selected for this evening's little adventure. They were the meanest and least intelligent cowboys on the Double D — men who would cheerfully kill somebody if there was twenty dollars in it for them.

'You boys know what's needful tonight?' asked Arkwright. 'Your fore-man here has explained the setup to you?' They all nodded and grunted. 'Just one thing to call to mind is that I don't want anybody hurt tonight. We might have to get up to those games in the future, but this evening, it's just a bit o' fun. You can set a few fires, trample crops, pull up fences, just make those squatters feel a mite scared, you get the picture?'

Stone himself said that he would lead the men on the expedition. He had confided in Arkwright that he didn't altogether trust them not to engage in rape and murder if there wasn't somebody present to call them to order.

Notwithstanding the fact that he had been the one to devise this latest scheme, Arkwright felt a twinge of misgiving, almost like a premonition of disaster. He shook himself impatiently. He was not a superstitious fool and no doubt he could rely upon Stone to ensure that things didn't get out of hand. He went back to the house, leaving the foreman to arrange the details of what was to be done.

Jed Stone had obtained a half-dozen white cloth bags and cut crude eye-holes in them. He showed these to the men who would be riding with him, saying, 'These here spook masks will stop us from being identified. It'll be dark, but there's no harm taking the precaution. 'Sides which, I've found as folk get more scared when they can't see faces. You know what some of those clods are like, they probably really believe in hants and suchlike.'

* * *

There were only four chairs in Zac's home and so the men crowding in were standing or sitting on the floor. Rose had taken their little daughter into the other room, to leave the men folk to talk. Apart from Bill Tucker and Zac, there were four other men. All farmed quarter sections nearby and every one of them was willing and able to stand up to any attempted intimidation by the boys from the Double D. They were not men who went looking for trouble, but neither were they the type to buckle under when threatened. They just wished to be left alone and not be interfered with.

Tucker hardly knew what to say when Zac invited him to stand forth and give his thoughts on the best way of combating the most powerful man for some miles around. He stood up, fearful of blushing like a schoolgirl, with every man's eyes upon him. After clearing his throat, he took a deep breath and was about to say the Lord knows what. He was in a way relieved when before he could even open his mouth, shooting erupted right outside.

8

Before setting off, there was some little debate between Stone and his men as to the best area to strike. Some of the boys were all for heading straight over to Indian Bluff and putting a scare into Bill Tucker. The fact that he had just shot a man dead gave this idea an extra spice which appealed to the more daring. Jed Stone said, 'No, the boss wants us to leave him be for now. 'Sides which, there's little enough point in riding down that way. Fisher and Logan are both dead and so their land is going to be freed up anyway. No, we'll go the other side of the bluff and see some of those livin' there. I heard that they are muttering about us and there's been some brave talk. Let's show 'em who's in charge round here.'

It was agreed in the end that the six of them would ride peaceably through the farms immediately adjacent to the Double D, round the back of the bluff and then descend like avenging angels on the squatters who lived up towards the foothills.

The half dozen riders cantered through the night, not talking but thinking about how they would play this. They were all of them bullies, including Jed Stone, men who preferred to pick on those who would not or could not fight back. Still and all, there was always the chance of some stray bullet finding its final resting place in one of your vital organs, when you were about these tricks and the awareness of this possibility had a sobering effect.

The troop of riders halted at the brow of a gentle slope which led down to the neatly tended fields below. Some of the men working this land had been here for over a year now; long enough to plough up the grassland and turn it into mud, which was wholly unsuitable for grazing cattle on. With luck though, all this land here, right up to the Rocky

Mountains, would soon be restored to its natural condition and life could return to normal. But first, they would have to demonstrate in a practical way to these damned sodbusters, just why they would be ill advised to hang round this corner of the territory for very much longer.

The shots, which sounded loud enough to be being fired right outside the very door of the soddie in which their meeting was being held, threw the men into consternation. It was one thing to sit over a pot of coffee and discuss in a casual way the defence of their land, quite another suddenly to find themselves under armed attack in this way.

To Bill Tucker, the shooting came as almost a pleasant surprise. He would a sight sooner engage in a gunfight than address a meeting. He had pulled the pistol automatically from his belt, before the echoes of the first shot had died down. Then he followed this up by doing something which looked to the others to be reckless and foolhardy, but was in fact a calculated risk. Tucker simply ran to the door and burst through it without pausing, out into the night.

Now the fact was, the men that Jed Stone was leading on this expedition had strict instructions not to harm anybody. Their aim was solely to put the fear of God into a bunch of dirt farmers. By sheer chance, Zac Hardy's place was the first they targeted for these games. Their intention was to whoop it up, fire a few shots into the air, burn a wagon or two, maybe even kill a horse or ox. Nothing too serious, just enough to get the message across that those men weren't welcome on the fringe of the Double D's range. They could just imagine the poor devil cowering within, with his arm round his wife and child perhaps, terrified out of his wits. This was the kind of bullying that these boys revelled in. They none of them expected for a moment to see the door fly open and a figure come sprinting out with a gun in his hand.

It had been Tucker's experience that when an assault was launched against a protected position, then those within tended to hunker down and fire from cover. The last thing on their minds, at least to begin with, was leaving shelter and engaging the besiegers out in the open. It was a simple psychological point, but of great importance at a time such as this. Later on, of course, those holed up might try and make a break for it. Maybe the attackers start a fire or bring up artillery or something; but that first instinct is to stay put. For this reason, the very last thing those outside are expecting is for anybody to come charging out soon after the first shots. In cases of this sort, the element of surprise was the most valuable of all.

As soon as he was out the door, Tucker saw that the riders milling about outside had torched Zac's wagon. So fierce was the blaze that he guessed, quite correctly, that they had probably poured a pint or two of lamp oil over the vehicle first. He didn't stop to examine that too closely though. He jinked from side to side, and ran to the little wooden shed in which he supposed Zac Hardy kept his grain, seed and tools. It was little bigger than a wardrobe, but large enough for Tucker to hide in the shadow of the thing.

The thing with firing off guns all over the place in the dark is, nobody can really tell if you are aiming them at anything special. Since there had already been two deaths in the area in the last few days, it would have been a rash man who chose to believe that the men wearing the spook masks, who had already set on fire Hardy's wagon, were only having a little high spirited fun. In fact, that was just about precisely what they were up to, but there was no way of knowing that, unless you had been present when they were given their orders. All of which explains why, as soon as Tucker was safely settled behind the shed, he drew down on one of the riders and shot him dead.

The men in Hardy's little house had been as shocked as the riders outside when they saw Bill Tucker dash through the door like that. When they heard, as they thought, the shooting starting up again, a few seconds after the man had run out, they roused themselves and drew their own pieces. Zac Hardy reached down the scattergun that was hanging from the wall and said, 'Well, I ain't about to let that fellow fight alone.' He too ran to the door, preparing for battle.

In a way, you could see where the men from the Double D were feeling a little vexed by developments. Here they were, just shooting the place up and starting a little fire and before you know it, men are shooting straight at them. When a second figure appeared in the doorway, illuminated from behind and silhouetted by two oil lamps, the reaction of two of the men was instinctive; they shot down Hardy before he had even a chance to fire his scattergun. Then Tucker fired once more and almost at once there came a perfect fusillade of shots from the windows of the soddie. Two more of the riders were hit, one being mortally wounded. It was enough. The remaining members of the party spurred on their horses and galloped off into the night, leaving one corpse and another man with perhaps ten minutes of life remaining to him.

The men from the Double D rode hard for ten minutes before Jed Stone called on them to rein in. They all pulled off their masks and looked at each other in dismay. What should have been little more than a display of high jinks had turned into something approaching a bloodbath. They were two men down and it was guessed that the man who had stood like that in the doorway with his gun in his hands had also been killed. It was the hell of a way to end what should have been an amusing adventure. The wounded man was in pretty good shape, a ball having merely grazed his upper arm.

Rose Hardy began weeping and wailing like a mad woman when she saw that her husband was dead. The other men tried to keep her from looking at the body, because one of the bullets had taken him through the eye and it was a right messy sight. She would not be gainsaid though and insisted on checking for herself that Zac was really dead. It was when she had established the fact that she was engulfed in a paroxysm of grief. Her child joined in and the men were left standing round uncomfortably as the two living members of the Hardy family bewailed the loss of a husband and father.

'He should have stayed inside,' observed Tucker in a low voice. 'Once I was out there, we could have caught them between two lines of fire. It was a good setup.'

'Can't be helped now,' said one of the men. 'You did what you could and we're right grateful. It might o' been worse.'

Another observed, 'You surely must

have nerves of steel to run straight into danger like that. I never saw the like.'

The truth was, at any other time Tucker would have been glowing with pleasure to hear himself being spoken of in such terms. As it was, the death of a man he had rather taken to and the realization that he had himself killed another man this night had cast him into something of a fit of dejection. Mind, he had agreed to take action and help organize things and he was not a man to break his pledged word. He accordingly asked if the four men present would favour him with their attention outside for a moment. When they were standing together, Tucker said, 'I'm sorry for the death of your neighbour. You all knowed him longer than me, I dare say, but what I saw in the short time I knew him, I liked. He will be missed. I stand ready to help though, if you men are still minded to resist any encroachment on your land.'

There were nods and grunts of agreement. The murder of Zac Hardy had had the effect of strengthening their resolve and all four of the men looked determined to fight. Tucker continued, 'The key to the matter is making sure that we are united. An attack on one man is an attack on us all. Any attack is like to come at night, like we just saw. I don't think those rascals durst be seen at their tricks in the broad light o' day. That bein' so, we must arrange to have a patrol out after dark, men such as can raise the alarm if they see anything amiss.'

'We're all workin' our land 'till whatever hour the good Lord sends us,' said one man. 'You telling' us we got to be out riding the range all night long as well? That's a hard row to hoe.'

'I don't say every man must be out, every night,' explained Tucker patiently. 'We'll need to be drawin' up a list. And we need more than just us five as well. If it comes to exchanging shots, then five of us against however many the Double D can muster ain't goin' to end well.'

As he reasoned out the case to them, Bill Tucker was astonished to hear himself speaking so firm and plain to men who didn't even know him. He wondered if they'd now tell him to get on out of there and tend to his own affairs, but none of them did. They appeared ready to accept his authority. Tucker didn't know it, but every one of those men had been mightily impressed to see him run straight out into what they took to be a hail of bullets. Such a man could not help but command a certain respect.

* * *

It was with some trepidation that Jed Stone knocked on the front door of Arkwright's imposing house to impart the sad news of the rout of their expedition. Arkwright didn't seem at all pleased to see him when he opened the door, saying grudgingly, 'Well, I suppose I have to invite you in. It's a wonder you don't just set up a camp-bed here and be done with it.'

Arkwright showed his foreman through to the kitchen and said, 'I guess you'll be wanting a drink. Hold hard a minute and I'll fetch you a whiskey.' Ushering Stone into the kitchen, rather than the parlour, was Septimus Arkwright's way of reminding the man where he stood in the scheme of things, which is to say a good few levels lower than his employer.

'So, what's the news?' asked Arkwright, as he handed the other man a glass. 'You put the fear o' God into them sodbusters?'

'Not exactly,' began Stone, preparing to prevaricate skillfully, but the boss of the Double D caught him up with the greatest irascibility.

'Not exactly?' cried Arkwright. 'Not exactly? What the hell are you talking about, man?'

'It's like this,' said the foreman, who then proceeded to outline the events of the night. When he had finished, there was silence for a space, before Arkwright asked who was killed.

'Geraghty and Anderson.'

'They have any identification on them?'

'Wouldn't have thought so,' said Stone. 'I don't see that this can be laid at our door. They could o' been riding with anybody.'

Privately, Jed Stone was amazed and relieved that the boss didn't show signs of anger at the awful mess that the raid had turned into. But Arkwright didn't have energy to waste on anger. His whole attention was focused upon that mortgage and his dwindling chances of getting the money to pay it off before the bank moved in and seized everything that he had spent his life building up.

'What's already happened can't be helped,' said Arkwright. 'It's what we do next as matters now. I won't deny as I'm a mite ticked off with that Bill Tucker. You think he had a hand in this night's work?'

'Hard to say, boss. Whoever come flying out that house was moving too quick in the darkness for to see his face.'

'All right, let's just forget this sorry business about those boys. Odds are, nobody'll tie them in with us, but even if they do, it don't signify. I want to talk now about getting ahold of that gold and we're going to do that tomorrow.'

'How's that?'

'Tucker's a no-count. There's nobody going to notice for a while if he drops out o' sight. I don't want his body turning up, mind, there's a deal too much killing taking place. Here's what I purpose that we should do tomorrow. And when I say 'we', that is as much as to say, I will be taking part myself. I can't trust you and those meatheads to do shit by your own selves. I will come along and show you how it is to be done.'

* * *

By the time he got back to his place and unrolled his blanket on the floor of his soddie, Bill Tucker was bone-weary. He was ready to go straight to sleep, but at the same time he felt restless. He was twitchy and anxious about what had chanced over at the Hardys' house and could not help but wonder if he should have done anything any different. Had he triggered the whole thing by running out in that way? But then, nobody had compelled those men to ride down on the place and begin loosing off firearms like that. They had been looking for trouble and sure enough, they had found it.

He stood up, went outside and began pacing up and down, his mind racing. The responsibility, which he had more or less accepted, of arranging patrols and guards for the district was weighing heavily upon Tucker. Hitherto, he had generally been a man who was told what to do by others. True, he had come out here to Wyoming to get away from being bossed around, but that didn't mean that he wanted to go to the opposite extreme and become one of those who ordered other people around. All he really hankered after was living his own life, with nobody interfering with him and he in turn leaving other folk's business alone.

It was while he was striding back and forth, that the idea came to Bill Tucker that the best way of tackling this might be to lay down his cards plainly and see what the other fellow had in turn — which meant going up to the Double D in the morning and speaking direct to Septimus Arkwright and asking him to leave them all alone and just concentrate upon his own land. The more that he thought about this, the better the notion seemed to be. If Arkwright knew that the homesteaders were not going to allow him to ride roughshod over them and that they were ready to defend their rights with lethal force, then maybe, just maybe, he would back off. It was surely worth a try.

★ ★ ★

Septimus Arkwright did not sleep well. His dreams were full of confused and disturbing images of tragedy and loss. More specifically, he dreamed that he was a hobo, on the road with no home and no money. He jerked awake from this nightmare, finding that he was covered in a slick of cold sweat. It was dawn, with the birds singing cheerfully and Arkwright knew that this was his last chance. If he and his men worked furiously for a week or so on Tucker's land, they might just unearth sufficient gold to pay off the mortgage. It was by no means certain that they would do so, but at least there was a chance. If they did not do that, then nothing was more certain than that in less than one calendar month, he would be bankrupt, with only the clothes on his back. There was no other choice; he would have to see Bill Tucker killed this very day and then begin looting his property the day after.

★　★　★

In contrast to the owner of the Double D, Tucker slept like a baby. Once he had decided what to do, he went back inside, rolled himself up in the blanket and then fell at once into a sound slumber. He too woke at dawn to the sound of the birds. It was the sweetest sound he ever heard in his life and reminded him at once that it was good to be alive.

The water in the stream seemed colder than ever as Tucker stripped to the waist and splashed himself all over his upper body. Lord, but it was good to be alive and to have your health. He wondered what time they rose on the ranch? He had an idea that they would be up bright and early, but then realized that although that might well be the case with the cowboys, such an important man as Arkwright would probably lay in bed a little later. Well, no matter, he had a lot to do himself today.

In fact, Tucker could have gone straight over to the Double D and found both Arkwright and Jed Stone up and about. The two men were in deep conference, leaning on a fence as though what they were discussing was of no great import.

'I don't want to be panning for little bits and pieces if we can help it,' Arkwright said. 'Going by the fact that you saw Tucker entering and leaving that sinkhole after dark, I'd say that he's found something there that he doesn't want folk to know of. Otherwise, why should he wait till the sun has set before going in?'

'You might be right,' said Stone. 'It's a strange thing to do else.'

'Might be right? Why, you know damn well I've hit the nail bang on the head. What other purpose could he have in stumbling up to that stream in the dark?'

'Happen you're right. How do we play it?'

'I don't want anybody 'cept you and me to know what becomes of Tucker. Soon as a man knows something relating to murder, he thinks as he has a hold over you. You and me, we know enough about each other not to fret overmuch about that.'

Stone tried to fathom out if this was an indirect threat, but so amiable was the boss this morning that he dismissed the thought. He said, 'So just you and me goin' to settle with that little bastard?'

'That's the boy! Yes, we'll do it neat and tidy so that nobody suspects aught and then put it about that Tucker sold out to us and has left the district.'

'Think folk in town'll buy it?'

'They won't even notice he's gone. I don't aim to put a notice about this in the newspapers, you noodle. It's just what we'll give out to the men here. If they ask, that is to say.'

*　*　*

It would take an hour and a half or so to walk to the Double D, but Bill Tucker was in a good mood and so had no objection to a brisk walk of that length. He was hoping to make a start on the blasting that evening, before going over the way and joining up with one of the other homesteaders to take first watch of the guard duty. He had been promised the loan of a horse and had engaged to spend from ten at night to two in the morning, criss-crossing the fields over towards where Zac had lately lived. Another two men would then take the four hours until dawn. If the men last night spoke truly, then they would be able to lay hands on others and the result would be that each man would only need to ride a four hour shift every third night. That was not too onerous.

Although he didn't look for any trouble up at Arkwright's place, Tucker had thought it wise to carry his pistol when he visited. He stopped for a moment to check that the mechanism was still smooth and the cylinder rolling easily. It was a fine weapon and he did not recollect having seen one blued in such a fashion. So dark was the colour that it looked almost black. He tucked the pistol back in his belt, making sure that it was loose and could be pulled without snagging.

* * *

Arkwright was standing at his ease, gazing out towards Indian Bluff, when he became aware of a figure marching towards him. When first he saw the man, he must have been a half mile or more away, but almost at once, Arkwright knew just who it was.

This promised to be at the very least an embarrassing encounter. There is bound to be something a little strained and odd about meeting and talking to a man you are determined to kill before the day is out.

9

From what he could see of it, the Double D looked to Tucker to be a well-to-do and prosperous spread. Indeed, they appeared to be doing so well, that he wondered that they wanted to start a range war against all the little farmers hereabouts. You would have thought that they would rather have adopted a policy of live and let live. That was by the by. Fact was, they did seem to want a range war and it was up to Tucker to warn them off, if he was able.

Three cowboys were leaning against a fence, watching Bill Tucker approach. They didn't know who exactly he was, but two things stood out about the man labouring up the slope in their direction. First off was that he clearly couldn't afford a horse. This alone made him something of a figure of fun to these men, who practically lived their lives on horseback. The other thing about him, which was obvious from his clothes, was that he was some no-count sodbuster. In general, the cowboys shared their boss's prejudice against the homesteaders and so they eyed the man heading their way in no friendly way.

Now for most of his life, Bill Tucker had had a mortal dread of encounters such as this. Three capable-looking young men sneering at him on account of his clothes, the way he walked or his general appearance — it was the sort of situation he would go far to avoid. In town, he might have turned a corner and gone the long way round to avoid loafers of this sort and the ridicule to which they might subject him. But something had changed within Tucker over the last few days. Perhaps it was finding that he owned a piece of land with gold on it or maybe it was the way that Zac Hardy and his neighbours had looked to him to provide a lead in their struggle with Arkwright and his boys. Could be that it was just that clear, fresh air which swept in from the Rockies and acted on him in the mornings like a tonic. Whatever it was, he was less apt to veer away from bullies than he had been when first he fetched up in Wyoming.

As he neared the three men, he sensed rather than heard that they had been talking about him and making a variety of uncomplimentary remarks on his appearance. Tucker nodded in a friendly enough way and continued on, heading for the big house.

'Morning, old-timer,' said one of the youths, all of whom were about twenty or thereabouts. 'You lost something?'

'Pardon me?' said Tucker.

'Must be deaf, as well as old,' remarked another of the boys, laughing. 'I don't know why they let those old men come out here to farm the land. As well as being a damned nuisance to the rest of us, it's just plumb cruel. Look at him, he can hardly make it up the hill.'

The others laughed and something about the sound of their laughter riled

Bill Tucker up. He had had more than enough mockery over the years to last him a lifetime. He stopped dead in his tracks, turned to face the three young men and said, 'I ain't looking for trouble, but if you boys want some, I've plenty and to spare.'

The agreeable way that the fellow said this, like he had too many apples and was offering to share them with his neighbours, meant that the three men leaning on the fence did not at first take his meaning. Then they saw the pistol tucked negligently in his belt. It was that dark in colour, that they had not before noticed it against his shirt and pants. Men in these parts were more apt to wear holsters when they were going heeled, not just stick a gun in the top of their pants like that.

When they realized that the old-looking farmer was in fact challenging them, the three slowly stood upright and moved away from the fence. Tucker was feeling almost as though he was liquored up. There was a recklessness upon him that he didn't rightly understand. It could be that having shot two men dead in as many days had given him a sense of his own prowess with deadly weapons. He had known that he was good with guns and explosives for many years, but had, since the war, avoided using this talent.

The three men facing him were still not sure of the play and didn't know whether this was about to turn into a gunfight. In truth, not a one of those boys had ever pulled his pistol in anger. They had none of them ever shot anything more menacing than a telegraph pole. While they were standing there uncertainly, Tucker suddenly drew the pistol from his belt and cocked it. The sharp, metallic click sounded deafening loud in the dead silence. Not one of the boys went for his piece and all stood like rabbits facing a fox with its teeth bared. Then the moment was over. Tucker pushed the Navy Colt back in his belt and remarked, in a friendly enough way,

'Lordy, you boys are slower than treacle.' Then he carried on past them, heading up to the house.

From the window of the parlour, Septimus Arkwright witnessed the whole scene. That little runt had faced down three of his men and could have killed them all into the bargain. And it was this man who would need to be disposed of if Arkwright had any hope of not ending up a beggar in the road. Tucker was heading straight towards him and was walking confidently up the steps to his house. With considerable reluctance, Arkwright went to the door to let him in.

'Why Mr Tucker, this is in the nature of a pleasant surprise. Won't you come in and set yourself down?'

'I ain't a stoppin' for a long chat, Mr Arkwright,' said Tucker quietly. 'I just thought it best were I to let you know what's what around here.'

The sheer breathtaking arrogance of it all but winded Septimus Arkwright. He had been in this district for over fifteen years and now this little fellow who only arrived last week was going to tell him what was what around here? The artificial smile on his face became frozen in a rictus as he ushered the homesteader through to the parlour. 'It's a little early for strong liquor, but I can offer you tea or coffee?'

'Nothing, thanks.'

'Well now, you were going to tell me what was what, is that how it is?'

'Yes,' said Tucker. 'I reckon that's about the strength of it. See now, Mr Arkwright, all this pushing and bullying that you and your men have been doin', with an aim to driving men from their land. It has to stop. There's been blood spilled and will be again. It will end badly.' Having said his piece, Bill Tucker didn't know what more to add. Then he said, 'I've kind of helped some of those living near here to organize. We'll be riding patrol from this coming night onwards. Any of your men come looking for fighting and such, they'll surely find it. I can't think that those livin' in Jubilee Falls will tolerate a regular war breaking out on their doorstep, as you might put it. It won't work, Mr Arkwright, so you'd best back off.'

Arkwright stared at the man as though he were a harbinger of doom sent by the Lord himself. In a few rough sentences, this fellow had summed up all that Arkwright had feared and also made it perfectly plain that he was the one at the back of the opposition to the interests of the Double D. He had arrived a few short days ago, a colourless little man who looked as though he was scared of his own shadow and wouldn't say boo to a goose. Now look at him, lording it round here like he was laying down the law. Well, the reckoning for such insolence would come this very night for this swaggering bantam cock. Arkwright hoped that none of these thoughts showed in his face as he said, 'I'm sorry you feel like that, Mr Tucker. I hoped that we could reach an accommodation.'

'How's that?'

'I had it in mind to offer you a price for your land. I'm not a hard bargainer, it would be worth your while.'

For a fraction of a second, the temptation was there to take Arkwright's money and just skedaddle out of there and start afresh elsewhere. But then, he had done this already in his life and more than once. They said that you packed your troubles with you in your bag when you ran away and over the course of his life, Bill Tucker had confirmed to himself the truth of this old saying. If he cut and ran again, then he would never get straight with himself. This was, in a sense, his last chance. All this went through his mind in a flash, which was strange in such a slow thinker. Then again, he recalled those men who were expecting him to ride out with them tonight to help guard their farms. It would be scurvy trick to run out on them as well. So he said, 'There's no price you could offer me, Mr Arkwright. Here I am and here I stay. Please remember though what I said. Don't trouble to show me out, I know the way.'

It had for many years been Septimus Arkwright's boast that he knew men. He used this as a knockdown argument if anybody queried some scheme of his or predicted aggravation from some quarter. Arkwright would say 'I know men' and that was an end to the question. The remarkable thing was that he was invariably right in his reading of the case. It seemed to those around him that Arkwright did indeed know men. For this reason, he was unusually perturbed as he stood at the window, watching Tucker walk away from the house. For here was a man who he did not know and could not understand.

Another of Arkwright's favourite sayings was 'Every man has his price', meaning that if you offer enough of the right thing, then everybody will forget their principles and throw their code of ethics overboard. But not this man. Here was somebody who apparently had no price. Of course, all the talk of offering to buy Tucker out had been bluff; he had no money to do anything of the kind. But Tucker couldn't know that. The biggest landowner for miles around had offered to buy his hundred and sixty acres and he hadn't even asked how much was on the table. Perhaps the man knew that the gold up by Indian Bluff made the land more valuable than Arkwright could afford? But deep in his heart, Septimus Arkwright knew that this was not the answer at all. Here was a man who was not affected by purely material considerations. He was being driven by some motive involving right and wrong or duty or some such foolishness. It was impossible to deal properly with such a fellow. Arkwright went to the door and opened it. Two hands were passing by towards the forge and he called out to them. 'One of you stop what you're about and find Stone. Tell him to come here at once.'

* * *

It was not at all uncommon for people to underestimate Bill Tucker and regard him as a fool. This was the mistake that Arkwright had made and as he trudged back towards the bluff, Tucker knew it. Even without knowing anything of the financial difficulties faced by the owner of the Double D, it was plain as a pikestaff that Arkwright was not offering to pay the market price for a stretch of land on which was to be found a reef of gold. That was all nonsense. The message that Tucker took away from the Double D that morning was that Arkwright had not the slightest intention of backing off and that if anything, he would be redoubling his efforts to dislodge the settlers from what he clearly regarded as his own land. So be it. He had done what he thought was needful and right by speaking to the man and setting out the case. If, despite this, he now wished to prosecute what was, in all but name, a war, then it would be upon his own head.

'Here's the deal,' said Arkwright. For the third time in recent days, his foreman was sprawling at his ease in the big house, admiring and envying the furnishings. 'We've reached the bone and there is no more room for manoeuvre. Tonight, you and me go up to the bluff and we take Tucker. I don't want any shooting. From what he tells me, there's some kind of guard being mounted from tonight and any gunshot will surely be the signal for a host of those scarecrows to come traipsing along to see what's happening.'

'No shooting? How'd you mean to take the fellow if we're unarmed?'

'I didn't say we'd be unarmed, by God. We'll have guns all right, but I hope not to use them. No, we'll take pick handles along of us and some rope. We're going on foot and I aim to arrive at that mud hut of Tucker's without any warning. Then we burst in, beat him senseless and then truss him up like a chicken.'

Jed Stone's unintelligent face lit up with simple pleasure. This was the kind of job he understood very well and enjoyed too. 'What then, boss?'

'Why, we take him to the stream and drown him. Then, once he's dead, we cut his bonds and throw the body into the sinkhole up by the bluff. I'll give out that I paid him for the mineral rights on his land this very day and hint that he's gone off on a drunk. Anybody finds his body, it'll look like he just fell over in the water and drowned. Any bruises we give him'll support that notion.'

'Then tomorrow, we start work?'

'Tomorrow, we start work. It's cutting it damned fine, but if, as I suspect, Tucker has found a good seam of gold in that cave, we should be able to get a hundred and fifty ounces out within a week or ten days. We'll just make it, you see if we don't.'

★ ★ ★

Of course, Tucker didn't know precisely how it would be attempted, but he certainly knew that Septimus Arkwright wanted his land. Obviously, he wanted all the land round here clear for his cattle, but he appeared to have a special and particular interest in this patch. Presumably, that was because he knew that gold had been found here and wanted to take it for himself. That was, thought Tucker sadly, often the way with rich men; they were frequently greedy as well as rich and wanted what other folk had as well. Maybe, he reflected, with sudden and unexpected insight, that's how they get rich in the first place, by always wanting other people's belongings and so on.

One thing you could bet on was that Arkwright wouldn't be making any move in daylight. No, Bill Tucker had until dusk to get on with his own work and then he would have to see about preparing for what might befall when night came. The main thing to get done was laying the charges in the cave. He was almost out of cash now and there was little prospect of making any more until he'd brought down that ceiling and could unload a few chunks of gold in town.

Originally, it had been Tucker's plan to detonate a few small charges and then keep checking at each stage how effective they had been. The more he thought about this, the more he had come to the conclusion that such a cautious approach was not necessary. In the worst case, he wasn't about to bring down the whole hillside into that sinkhole. He might collapse more of the ceiling than was needed, but that wouldn't be a disaster. After all, whatever fell down would create a corresponding gap above. He wasn't going to block the cave up entirely. Even if he brought down a few tons of limestone, he would be able to clear it away easy enough. It would all be in broken fragments. Anyway, it might reveal more of that enormous vein of gold that was clearly running through the rock.

It was this reasoning that caused Tucker to pour about a quarter of the powder in that fifteen-pound keg out into an old tin box and set it to one side, and then work on the remainder as being his charge. He knew the very spot to place it, too — the deep cleft that he had found, the one that he could thrust his arm in without coming to the back of it. He thought that he remembered a boulder jammed in there as well, which would provide a convenient platform for this keg.

The keg, he wrapped in a quantity of tar-paper and then enveloped the whole in some oil cloth, which he sealed neatly with a few pins. Tucker gave some thought to the length of fuse needed and finally settled upon two foot. That would give him time to be completely clear of the mouth of the sinkhole when the charge blew. He surely to God didn't want to be in that tunnel when twelve pounds of fine grained black powder went up!

Before setting out the cave, Tucker scanned the bluff for any sign of spies. From all that he was able to collect, there was not a living soul watching his actions and so he carried the keg, fuse and his storm lantern down to the water's edge and strolled along until he came to the sinkhole. He didn't linger outside, but just took off his boots and waded right into the water.

Just as he had remembered, the deep cleft had a largish rock jammed into it, the surface of which was three foot clear of the water. It was bone-dry there, no splashes reached this high. Although the cave had overall a clammy and moist feel to it, Tucker figured that his keg and fuse should be all right for a few hours until tonight, when he sprang his mine and saw what chanced. He glanced longingly up at the ceiling; tantalizingly out of his reach. The gleaming yellow that he could see in the lamplight would be enough to solve all his difficulties.

* * *

The afternoon dragged for both Septimus Arkwright and Bill Tucker. In the hearts of both was a suppressed excitement, a sense that everything was coming together nicely. For Tucker, this was the expectation that an hour after the sun set, he would be filling his pockets with as much gold as he could pick up with his two hands. There was also the fact that he was going to stand guard later that night with men who regarded him with respect and looked to him as some kind of leader. This was a matter of great wonder to Bill Tucker; such a thing had never before in his life been known. He was determined to show himself worthy of the trust which those men were evidently prepared to give him.

Over at the Double D, Arkwright was also excited, although in his case this excitement was almost in the nature of fever. His eyes were glittering and he found at odd times that his hands were trembling. Everything rode on this night's work. His home, his livelihood, everything would be decided within a few hours. He was like a man at a gaming table who has bet his home on the turn of a card or roll of the dice. As Arkwright loaded his rifle, his hands were shaking so badly that he had to stop for a moment and take a few deep breaths, he was spilling that much powder everywhere.

Jed Stone was not an imaginative man and although he knew, in an abstract way, that if Arkwright went down, he would go down with him, this was only a vague and insubstantial notion. Stone was a man for whom only the here and now really mattered. He was like the fellow in scripture who gave no thought to the morrow. Jed Stone knew only what he could see, hear and feel right now. The only part of the projected activity which had caught his fancy was the idea of drowning Bill Tucker. He had never killed a man by drowning and it might prove a pleasing novelty.

10

Nobody's plans went as they were meant to do that night. To begin with, Tucker did not, as might reasonably have been expected by those seeking him, remain in or around the vicinity of his soddie. He was in a thoughtful mood, not common to him, and had a fancy to see the sun set from high up on Indian Bluff. Everything had been happening at breakneck speed over the last week or so and he felt in need of a little calm reflection. He didn't carry anything up there, other than his pistol, tucked carefully into his belt; he would go back and get his lantern later, when it was time to blow that charge. So it was that as the sun set, Tucker was perched a hundred feet above the stream, his thought straying who knows where.

Arkwright had brought a lamp with

him. After they had disposed of Bill Tucker, he wanted to have a poke about in that sinkhole that his foreman had seen Tucker coming out of, the night Logan was killed. It was Arkwright's aim that a gang of his men should fetch up here at dawn and begin work immediately. If he had already scouted out the limestone cave and found out any visible seams of ore, then it would mean the job could get going all the quicker.

As they approached the bluff, Arkwright and Stone dismounted. They led their mounts along for a while, until they were actually in sight of Tucker's soddie, which was some mile off. The daylight was fading fast, but the moon was already on the rise. They secured the horses to a couple of pine trees and then walked on.

Tucker had gained real pleasure from watching the sun sink below the horizon. People were, he thought, usually too busy and full of their own concerns to spend time taking in such a sight. It had acted on him like a tonic and he felt braced and ready for the lively night ahead. After he had blown that charge, he would have a few hours to investigate the consequences, before he had promised to go on patrol with the others. It was when he was almost at the bottom of the bluff, after slithering and sliding down like a school boy, that he caught sight of the two men walking towards his home. Even at this distance, they had a slinking, furtive air and as soon as he set eyes upon them, Tucker knew they were up to no good.

Arkwright and Stone were each carrying both a rifle and a pick handle. They hoped to take their target unawares and beat him senseless, without making any noise about it. When they reached the soddie, they walked quietly round to the back and waited there for a little while, listening. There was no sound and so Arkwright tapped the foreman's arm and indicated that they should move round to the front and rush in. They propped their rifles carefully against the back wall of the soddie and Arkwright set down the lantern he was carrying.

There was no door yet to Tucker's soddie, just an old Indian blanket hanging in the doorway, the primary function of which was to keep out the wind and rain and provide the hut's occupant with some degree of privacy. The two men tore aside the blanket and rushed into the hut. It was empty. Then, from a distance, they heard a man cry, 'You men had best throw down your weapons. I got you covered good!'

From that distance, Tucker couldn't have taken oath as to the identities of the two men who had charged into his home, but he was sure in his own mind that it was Arkwright and his foreman. Although he was possessed of an exceedingly equable temperament, the casual way that those fellows were entering his property had roused Bill Tucker to something approaching real anger. He had gone as far as he could to avoid a showdown, but if this is what they would have then so be it.

One good thing about working with Jed Stone was that when things got rough, you didn't need to explain to him what was needed. Arkwright ran from the hut and swerved round at once, heading for where he had left his rifle round the back. Stone did just exactly the same thing, simultaneously. This left the two of them, armed to the teeth, firing from cover. They didn't know at this point how many men they might be facing, but they were surely in a good position. Arkwright was thinking about these patrols that Tucker had told him of and wondering if he was facing a dozen armed men. He was relieved when he peered cautiously round the edge of the turf wall and saw that it was just one lone figure standing there. He called, 'Tucker, is that you?'

'Yes, it is. You best throw down any guns you got, Mr Arkwright. I ain't in a mood for foolin', I tell you straight.'

Despite their hope of settling with Tucker quietly, without recourse to firearms, that was obviously out of the question now. Arkwright took careful aim and fired at the man standing there in the twilight. Tucker dropped down, but whether because he had been hit or on account of not wanting to be such a clear target, it was impossible to say.

As soon as the men behind his soddie opened fire, Tucker knew that the best he could do was just drop right down and lay prone. They would hardly be able to see him in the gloom and at this range. He took rough aim at the side of the building where he had seen the flash of fire. There was one good thing about this business, apart that is from bringing the whole thing out into the open, and that was that it had been agreed with the others that any gunshot would be investigated. That might not be soon enough to help him, but it would mean that those two villains wouldn't get away with this. He calculated that it would take a half-hour for the men over by Zac Hardy's district to gather themselves together. Say another half-hour to get here. Could he hold Arkwright and the other fellow at bay for that long? They would have to see.

'What do you think?' asked Stone. 'Think you hit him? Or is he shamming?'

'I couldn't say, Jed. One thing's for sure, we can't stay here all night. If I know how these things work, him and those others will have arranged that any shooting be the sign for a muster of their patrol or whatever you care to call it. We have to deal with him pretty damned quick.'

'I'll make a sprint to that ox cart and see if he fires,' Stone said. 'Least that way, we'll know if he's still in action.'

Jed Stone did not hang around, when once he had something to undertake. He had no sooner spoken, than he ran to the cart, which was twenty yards from the soddie. Tucker fired twice at him, but in the uncertain light, both shots were wide of the mark. They provided valuable information to the two men intent on killing him though. They could tell at once that Tucker was firing a pistol. Arkwright had marked the weapon when Tucker came calling earlier that day and knew it to be a cap and ball model Colt. Unless Bill Tucker was a complete fool and went round with the hammer resting on a live chamber, that meant that he had only three shots left and no chance of reloading in a hurry. Even if he had a flask of powder near at hand and a bunch of caps, he wouldn't have the time. Arkwright thought that he better not give the man any leisure to do so, just in case and leaned round the corner and fired in the general direction of Tucker, who fired back at once. Two shots left.

Bill Tucker had been carrying out precisely the same calculations in his own head and knew that his only hope was to make a run for it. There were two men, one crouched behind his ox cart and the other at the back of his hut. They'd had no chance to reload their rifles, which meant that like him, they were firing pistols. Unlike him though, they would have five shots a piece in their guns; ten shots to his two.

If he began running from here, and made sure to change direction a lot, he would be sure to make it to the stream. The others wouldn't be able to fire while they were running. First, he had to get them both to duck down, to give him a chance to get somewhat of a lead on them. He fired once at the cart and once at the corner where the other man had been firing from and then sprang to his feet and made for the stream.

It took a second or two for Arkwright and Stone to realize what was happening and then they both began chasing Tucker. It was a perfect setup, just the way that the two of them liked it. Their quarry was effectively unarmed and all they had to do was run him down and then finish him off.

He was panting for breath by the

time he reached the water's edge. This time, Tucker didn't bother to remove his boots, but plunged straight into the water and disappeared into the sinkhole.

'We got him, Jed,' said Arkwright, with enormous satisfaction. 'We got the bastard like a rat in a trap. He's got no more shots left and there's two of us with guns. There's no way out of that tunnel, I suppose?'

'Not that I ever heard of.'

'Right, let's finish this now, before anybody shows up. You set right here, while I go and fetch that lamp. You see hide nor hair of that man, just shoot him down, you hear what I say?'

'I got that.'

Having been in the cave a few times with his lantern, Tucker knew the place well enough to move along a bit in the pitch dark. He had a packet of Lucifers in his pocket, but he wasn't about to strike one just yet awhiles. If either of those men were peering in, it would simply give them a target. He plodded slowly and carefully onwards, feeling the ceiling with his hands, so that he would know as soon as he emerged into the larger cavern with the seam of gold. It might end with his own death too, but Bill Tucker was damned if he was going to lay down and die for those two devils. He had the makings of a plan.

After he had fetched the lamp from where he left it, back of Tucker's soddie, Arkwright made his way back to the entrance to the cave. As he approached the spot where Jed Stone was standing guard, he had made his mind up about how to play this. There was little time, if his guess was right and their shooting had attracted unfavourable attention. They had to kill Tucker real fast and then dig up, so as to be gone when anybody came by to look into the gun battle. 'No sign of him?' Arkwright asked when he reached Stone.

'Not a peep.'

'Here's what we do. We got a lantern and we will follow Tucker's trail. We're sure to see him ahead of us and he will be as helpless as a rabbit. I've been in caves like this before. They might be wide enough at the mouth, but they soon narrow down. We ain't going to have to follow him for a mile, nor nothing like it.'

★ ★ ★

The ceiling rose until it was quite out of reach of his questing fingertips, by which Tucker knew that he was in what he thought of as the main cavern. He felt his way along to the right carefully, until he found the cleft in which he had stowed the keg of powder. Very carefully — it would be a disaster were he to knock it into the water — he found the slick oil cloth surrounding the charge. The fuse was still dry and all was set for him to set a light to it. Tucker took the packet of Lucifers out and extracted one.

Outside, at the entrance to the sinkhole, Septimus Arkright was lifting the glass chimney and lighting the lamp. It cast a cheerful, ruddy glow upon the scene. He said, 'Listen now. We both have our guns at the ready. He can't get away from us, we know as he is trapped in that cave. It's only a matter now of running him to earth.'

'He's apt to get vicious when he's cornered,' remarked Jed Stone, his view based upon long experience. 'Even the mildest of men can get downright dangerous when they got their backs to the wall.'

'I mind we've got enough viciousness between the two of us to counter any we find in another,' said Arkwright shortly. 'Come, we'd best finish this as soon as may be.' The two of them stepped into the stream and began wading into the cave.

Bill Tucker could see the light in the distance and the indistinct shapes of the two men who were coming, without the least atom of a doubt, to kill him. Their shadows flickered and flared before them, like something from a bad dream. He would have to time this just right. On the one hand, it wouldn't do to let those fellows catch sight of him. They would start shooting as soon as there was so much as a glimpse. Then again, he didn't want to set the fuse too early and have the thing go off when they were too far away. It would take the most perfect timing. Tucker crouched down so low that his butt was in the water.

The two men came on slowly and cautiously. Notwithstanding the fact that they knew the man they were hunting did not have a loaded weapon, they were both of them canny enough to know that a man with his back to the wall might still come up with a few tricks. He might not be in a position to shoot them, but that didn't mean that Bill Tucker couldn't spring out with a knife in his hand or shy rocks at their heads.

Arkwright signalled to his companion to stop for a moment and they both listened carefully. There was nothing to be heard. Then, just a little way ahead of them, there was a sudden and urgent splashing, like somebody was running as fast as he could in water which came up to his knees. They both began moving as quickly as they were able towards the source of the sound.

11

At what he gauged to be the last possible moment, Tucker struck the Lucifer, taking care to shield its light within the cleft. He lit the fuse and then, after dropping the spent match in the water, jumped up and began running as fast as he was able through the water. He had not explored any further than this section of the cave and would just have to hope that the ceiling didn't suddenly come down to a few inches above the surface of the water. If it did, then he was a dead man.

As Arkwright and Stone entered the larger cavern, the light of the lamp which the owner of the Double D was carrying flooded the place, reflecting from the surface of the water and sending dancing beams of light upwards to the ceiling overhead. Arkwright glanced up and then stood stock still, forgetting for a moment that he was in hot pursuit of a man he wished to kill. 'God almighty,' he cried, awestruck. 'Will you just look at that!'

Stone too looked up and was also transfixed by the sight of so much glittering wealth, hanging above their heads like the stars of the night sky. It was in that attitude, with both men overcome by greed and struck speechless by the sight of such riches, that death found them — when twelve pounds of fine grained black powder exploded just ten feet from where they were standing.

*   *   *

The blast from the explosion hurled Tucker forward into the water. The shock wave, magnified tenfold in the narrow confines of the tunnel, sent him tumbling along, head over heels in the darkness. Somehow, he avoided dashing out his brains on the rocky walls. When he lay still, he found that he was actually submerged and in a panic reared up from the water like a sea monster. The air was so full of dust that he was hardly able to breathe and he untucked his shirt from his pants and held it over his mouth as an improvised mask or filter. This seemed to help a little and although the bone-numbing cold from the water in which he squatted was seeping into him, he kept this position for some while.

Eventually, he fancied that the air was clearing a little and ventured to uncover his face. Tucker found that he could breathe more easily and he stood up. For a moment, he panicked and feared that he would not be able to judge which was the way out of the cave. For a split second, he had a vision of himself, wandering ever further into the limestone tunnel, until perhaps he found himself beneath the distant Rocky Mountains. Then his common sense asserted itself and he decided to walk for the count of a hundred in one direction and then, if he had not found himself in the large cavern where he could not feel the ceiling, he would turn back and try the other way.

Fortunately, he chose right the first time and long before he had reached a hundred, he felt the ceiling fall away and he found himself in a large, open chamber. Forgetting the damage that might have been wrought by his mine, he walked on confidently, only to stumble and fall against a wall of jagged rocks which had not previously been there. He felt with his hands and was horrified to find that the broken stone seemed to form an almost vertical wall, blocking his path entirely. The water was growing deeper here and he knew that he had created some sort of dam, preventing the water from flowing out.

'This is a damned tricky business,' he muttered out loud. Then he recalled his earlier thoughts on the subject and knew that however much rock had come cascading down, it must perforce have created a corresponding space above. He began slowly scrambling up the heap of boulders; despite his sound reasoning, he was fearful of finding that his way would be blocked by the ceiling of the tunnel and that he would be entombed here.

Tucker needn't have worried. Most of the force of the blast must have been funnelled sideways, rather than to the roof. He guessed that he had to scramble no more than ten or twelve feet before coming to the top of the heap of broken limestone. He slithered down the other side and then made his way carefully to the exit of the cave. He surely had dammed the stream, because he found himself wading not through water, but mud. He wondered what would happen to all that pent up water, in the end. Would the force of it cause the wall of rocks to give way?

As he stumbled gratefully out of the sinkhole and into the fresh night air, Tucker was astonished to hear a voice cry, 'Stand to! Make a move and we'll shoot you down like a dog.' He froze into immobility, not daring to think what would happen next. Then, to his relief, another voice said:

'Why, you damned fool. Put up your weapon. That there's Mr Tucker.'

He found that five men were clustered around the entrance to the cave; all pointing their guns in his general direction. Four of the men he recognized, having seen them at Zac Hardy's home. They were staring at him like he was a ghost. Tucker said, 'I'm mighty grateful to you boys for turning up like this. I mind though that we won't need to worry any further.'

'We heard a heap of shooting and then mustered and came running,' said one of the men. 'Just as we arrived, there was the most great rumble beneath our feet and then a cloud of smoke and dust came out of that hole. We suspicioned as something was going on and it took no great thought to conclude that the Arkwright fellow was at the back of it.'

'Well, you're nearly right,' said Tucker. 'Fact is though that Arkwright and his deputy have fallen victim to what I suppose you could call a mining accident. I laid a charge and then they come blundering along, trespassing on my land, and ran right into it. It's tragic, but when you go interfering with folk's land like that, it oftentimes ends badly.'

The five men looked at Bill Tucker, wondering if he was going to explain further. When he kept silent, they looked away and one man said, 'I guess you're right. You say as they were trespassing and have been killed, I think the blame falls on their heads alone.'

It was clear that the group of them were pleased to hear of Arkwright's demise, but felt that it would be in poor taste to gloat about it. With expressions of good will, they parted amicably from the man who had freed them from the shadow under which they had been living for some little while. They had the air of men who owed a debt of gratitude and Tucker had the idea that if he needed any help and assistance in the future, those boys would fall over themselves to provide it.

It was late and after the experiences of the last hour or so, Tucker didn't feel inclined to go checking out the sinkhole further that day. No doubt, he would have a lot of digging and excavation to carry on in that tunnel. Unless he missed his guess badly, the gold would be buried under several tons of rock and it would need a deal of work to bring it out.

When he woke the next morning, his back ached and he had earache. It didn't feel to Tucker like he had done himself a serious mischief, but all the same, he thought it best not to go delving about in his cave just then. Instead, he rooted about and found that he still had nearly three dollars in loose coins. Would that be enough to buy a pickaxe? The only way to find out was to walk to Jubilee Falls and ask Mr McAllister. There was also the matter of reporting Arkwright's death to somebody. He didn't see that he could rightly be blamed for what had happened, but at the very least, he should, he supposed, notify somebody.

By the time he got to town, Tucker was aching all over. Perhaps being in the close proximity to such a blast was an experience to be avoided in the future, he thought. McAllister was happy to sell him a pickaxe for just over a dollar and as he was about to leave the shop, he said tentatively, 'I don't expect, Mr McAllister, you would know who I ought to report a death to?'

'Weell now, that all depends who's dead,' said the shopkeeper, 'and how they died, ye ken. Are ye wantin' to tell me the story?'

Briefly, and leaving out a good deal, Bill Tucker told McAllister about the incident in the cave. After he had finished, the Scotsman sucked in his breath and mulled over what had been said. Then he spoke. 'I'm thinkin' ye left much from your account. I dare say ye've your reasons. As to who ye should tell, well I'm as good a man as any. Did ye not know I'm head o' our vigilance committee?'

'I didn't know that.'

'Aye well, that'll be 'cause ye don't live in town. Still, there it is. I'll spread the word. And strictly between the two of us, Mr Tucker, I doot there'll be a lot of grievin' for Septimus Arkwright. There's been trouble brewin' and maybe now it's been nipped in the bud.'

Walking back, with the pickaxe over his shoulder, Tucker thought that everything was more or less cleared up. With Arkwright and Stone dead, there would be nobody to lead the men at the Double D and the enterprise might just fall apart of its own accord. More to the point, he was himself a fabulously wealthy man now. He would begin this very afternoon the task of clearing away the debris from the explosion. There was enough gold buried under those chunks of shattered limestone to mean that he would never have to work again for the whole course of his life.

After he had wolfed down a hunk of

stale bread, Tucker could wait no longer. He topped up the reservoir of the storm lantern and lit it, then made his way down to the stream, carrying with him his spade and the new pickaxe which he had acquired that very day. There was one aspect of the digging which really did not appeal to him and that was the fact that beneath all those tons of rock were the bodies of two men. They might, in life, have been villains, but it was not pleasant to recall that he had himself killed them, and Tucker supposed that he would have to haul out the corpses and make some provision for their disposal. The sooner they were removed the better; they would in a day or two be fouling the water of the stream.

The water was flowing again, so presumably it had found a way through the barrier of fallen rock. Tucker took off his boots and then began working his way up towards the chamber which contained the gold. When he got there, he discovered that the force of the water building up had acted to dislodge the loose rocks, carving a channel in the middle of the dam. He arranged some of the rocks like a little ledge and set the lamp there. Then he began digging.

At first, Tucker enlarged the gap for the water to flow through. Then, he began to move stones to one side in order to reach the precious metal which must have fallen from the ceiling. Looking up, he could see the glint of the seam, where it had been broken off. Lord, he thought to himself, there must be countless pounds of the stuff in this cave. It's a real Eldorado.

After a half hour of digging, he saw something shining, right where he had been swinging his pick. It was a lump of shining metal, about as big as a plum. Tucker was feeling all over aches and pains and thought that he would call it a day. There was surely enough in that one lump to keep him going for a while without worrying about financial difficulties. He moved a couple of large stones to one side and pulled out the nugget.

Then, he picked up his tools, collected the lamp and made for the daylight.

Once out of the cave, Tucker sat down on the bank of the stream and examined his prize. It was then that an awful fear assailed him. Surely, this was lighter than it should be? The other chunks of gold had weighed about the same as pieces of lead of similar size would have done, but that wasn't at all the case with this nugget. In a panic, he jumped into the stream and lifted out two smooth rocks. He brought them to the side and placed the gold on one of them. Then he brought the other rock crashing down as hard as he could. The gold shattered into half a dozen fragments. It was only then that it dawned on him that all this fuss, the murders and all the rest of it, had been over a reef of iron pyrites or fool's gold. There had never been any gold in that cave.

He sat there for a space, stunned and incredulous; sick to his stomach. Then he rallied. Of course there was gold in the case. Hadn't he picked it up himself from this very stream and sold it for a good price in town? There must be both pyrites and gold, mixed up together. In a frenzy he rushed off to the spot where he had collected the gold. There could not be the least doubt that gold had been carried by the water to this spot and if not from the cave, then where?

Tucker got into the stream and began feeling the bed with his fingers. How had that gold come to be trapped here and only here? It was then, as he was bending down and rubbing his hands over the stones of the stream bed, that a gleam of gold caught his eye. It wasn't in the water though; it was in the shadow of the mossy old log, sticking out from the earth beneath it.

None of this made any sense at all and Tucker reached under the log to pull out the nugget. It was a substantial one, weighing, from what he could tell, nearly an ounce. How the devil had it come to be lodged right up here though, on the bank? It was so heavy, that however fast the water was flowing, it would not have bounced and jumped up here.

Peering under the log, Tucker thought he could see another piece of gold, he reached into the space and plucked out another nugget, smaller than the first. There looked to be something more under the log, but he wasn't likely to see what, without shifting the tree trunk itself. Tucker went back to where he had left the pickaxe and then commenced work; hacking away at the earth beneath the great log. He worked slowly and carefully, because he kept finding other little pieces of gold, embedded in the mud. After an hour, he had revealed a hollow containing some mouldering clothes and a human skeleton. The skeleton had been picked altogether clean and white by animals and insects and Tucker felt no revulsion for these mortal remains. He had no idea how long they had been laying here; long enough to rot away the garments which the person had worn, certainly.

Beneath the skeleton was a leather pack which, although showing signs of having been gnawed at by mice or rats, appeared to be largely intact. Carefully, Tucker tugged it out. He didn't like the notion of looting a dead man's belongings, but there was a mystery here which needed to be solved. The contents of the pack did not at first promise to shed any light on the matter. Soggy paper, the writing on it obliterated by years of damp, a rusty pistol of antiquated design and a little glass bottle, with a stopper also made of glass. The label on the bottle was faded away almost to nothing, but by holding it close to his eyes, Tucker could just make it out. It said, in very old fashioned script, 'Aqua Fortis'. Something about those words rang a bell.

The only other things in the pack were a small hammer of curious shape and unknown purpose and a piece of flat, black stone about three inches long. It was this piece of stone which triggered the memory in Tucker's mind as to where he had encountered the words 'Aqua Fortis'. It had of course been in Carl Halliday's shop, when he was showing how to test for gold. He had also had a black stone, just like this one. The full implication took a while to sink in and when it did, Bill Tucker felt quite crushed.

All this whole to-do about gold had been a mare's nest. There never had been any gold here, other than that dropped by this long-dead prospector. He must have died or been killed here and somehow some of his gold had found its way into the nearby stream. It had all been for nothing. He, Bill Tucker, was no richer now than he had been when he fetched up here.

For nearly half an hour, Tucker sat brooding about his misfortune. That is to say, to begin with he thought about his misfortunes, but by and by, he started to count his blessings. It was true that he was not likely to become a wealthy man from the amount of gold found here. On the other hand, there was quite a bit of gold beneath and around the skeleton. He'd be surprised if it all added up to less than sixteen ounces. That would bring him, what, three hundred dollars? Enough, without a doubt, to tide him over for a while. And of course, he still had almost a hundred acres of land, with a good source of water running through it.

Then again, for a short while, he had been a person of consequence in these parts. He had had land that people wanted, as well as which, a band of men had looked to him, Bill Tucker, to lead them. That was something to remember with pride. Slowly, his perspective on the business shifted, until he began to think that he hadn't done too badly, after all. He had come here to work the land and that was what he would do. He was three hundred dollars better off than he had been and had made some friends hereabouts who would probably lend him a helping hand if he needed it. He didn't think either that anybody in this district would have him marked down as a man to be bullied or pushed around. Quite the reverse, in fact.

Tucker stood up. It had been fun to play at being a fabulously rich man, but he never really saw himself in that character. He guessed that he would have to work for his living, same as he always had. Well, there was nothing to grieve about in that; most everybody had to work. He picked up the gold that he had found and stowed it in his pockets. Then, Bill Tucker set off to harness up that plough. He had wasted a lot of valuable time over this nonsense and the sooner he got to work, the better.

We do hope that you have enjoyed reading this large print book.

Did you know that all of our titles are available for purchase?

We publish a wide range of high quality large print books including:
Romances, Mysteries, Classics
General Fiction
Non Fiction and Westerns

Special interest titles available in large print are:
The Little Oxford Dictionary
Music Book, Song Book
Hymn Book, Service Book

Also available from us courtesy of Oxford University Press:
Young Readers' Dictionary
(large print edition)
Young Readers' Thesaurus
(large print edition)

For further information or a free brochure, please contact us at:
Ulverscroft Large Print Books Ltd.,
The Green, Bradgate Road, Anstey,
Leicester, LE7 7FU, England.
Tel: (00 44) 0116 236 4325
Fax: (00 44) 0116 234 0205

RIDING FOR JUSTICE

Ben Bridges

The mining town of King Creek sits in the heart of the Nevada goldfields. It has no law to speak of but Stover's Law — ruthlessly enforced by one greedy woman, her three callous sons, and a dozen hired gunmen. The Stover family is systematically fleecing the townsfolk of everything they have, with anyone standing in their way either bought off — or killed off. In desperation, Pearl Denton turns to her old friend, legendary town-tamer Sam Judge, for help . . .

SAVAGE

Jake Henry

In 1864, Captain Jeff Savage is tasked with taking down Carver's Raiders, a ruthless bunch of killers who have blasted a bloody path through the Shenandoah Valley. The mission is a failure, and Carver escapes with a handful of men. Two years later, he and his gang rob a bank in Summerton, murdering Savage's wife Amy. Several outlaws escape in the aftermath: armed with their names, Savage sets out to track each one down and exact his revenge . . .

THE SHOESTRINGERS

C. J. Sommers

Benjamin Trout, foreman of the K/K Ranch, has been cut loose for being too old — while Eddie 'Dink' Guest, a new hire, has been fired for being too young. With nowhere to go, both ride out together to seek work elsewhere. When they encounter widowed Beth Robinson and her daughter Minna in the wilderness, they are invited back to the women's ranch — and become the Robinsons' allies in the struggle to save their land from the predatory Cyrus Sullivan.

DEAD MAN DRAW

Walt Keene

Retired lawman Dan Shaw and veteran gunfighter Tom ride into the sprawling town of Dead Man Draw. Quickly hired as sheriff and deputy, and charged with collecting protection money from town businesses, it doesn't take long to discover why their appointments were so hasty — the place is crawling with hired killers, and two drifters are considered expendable. But these old-timers have an ace in the hole — their friend Wild Bill Hickok has their backs . . .

PROFESSOR HAYES

Billy Moore

'Professor' A.J. Hayes is hired to serve as a teacher in San Juan, where he manages to upset the community by not only instantly wedding Rachel McNew — a young woman arriving on a marriage train — but disciplining the son of Curt Tucker, the local mine owner, and brawling with Tucker in public. Fired from the school, A.J. and Rachel — still happily married despite everything — move to a cabin in a valley. But their new life together is soon under threat . . .